THE LIFE OF CHIBUOGWUM

S.O. OGBONNAYA

PHOENIX VOICES PUBLISHING

CONTENTS

CHAPTER ONE

Mr. Okereke and his wife, Uloaku sat in the headmaster's office with the headmaster and their son, Chibuogwum.

"I am happy that you are here today following my invitation that you should come and see me," the headmaster, Mr. Anyansi said, thanking Mr. Okereke and his wife, Uloaku. "I am so grateful to you that you made time out of your busy schedules to honour my invitation."

"We thank you too for welcoming us well," Mr. Okereke replied.

"I invited you here because I and my teachers are overjoyed over your son's good behaviour and excellent performances in his academics. We are very proud of him. We know that you are the source of his good behaviours. I know that it is because of the good trainings you give him at home together with instructions we are giving him here that contributed to his good characters. So, I urge you to keep it up."

He turned to Chibuogwum and said "My child, I heartily congratulate you on your excellent performances in your subjects."

"Thank you, Sir," Chibuogwum answered.

"As we all know," the headmaster said, "Chibuogwum applied to be admitted into the prestigious Echianu High School.

And as we also are all aware, Echianu High School only takes pupils whose academic performances are high and satisfactory. So, getting admitted into the school is not easy." The headmaster, Mr. Anyansi paused. "However," he went on, "Once again, I congratulate you, Chibuogwum. You performed so well in the school's entrance examinations, and you have been offered admission to study at Echianu High School. Come and have a handshake."

Chibuogwum got up from where he was sitting between his parents and went to the headmaster and they warmly shook hands, the headmaster smiling at Chibuogwum.

As the headmaster was yet holding Chibuogwum's hand, he said: "You have made this school proud. You scored 90% in the exams. That means that you had the highest score among all the pupils from more than thirty schools that partook in the entrance examinations organised by Echianu High School. So, you have been accepted into the school for your secondary school education.

Chibuogwum was so happy and he smiled. The headmaster smiled too.

"I have a few words of advice for you, my child," the headmaster continued.

"You began well with us and ended excellently with us. However, I will advise you to continue to be of good behaviour and avoid bad friends who may influence you negatively. Throughout your stay with us in this school, you have always maintained your good name and fear of God, and you are also diligent in your studies. I will like to hear as you go out of this school, that you continue to walk on that road. I wish you the best as you start your secondary school journey."

"Thank you very much, sir. "I am promising you that I will continue to be well-behaved even as I leave this school to enter secondary school," Chibuogwum pledged.

Chibuogwum was so happy for the news that he had been offered admission into Echianu High School for his secondary school education. Every pupil in the area dreamed of attending Echianu High school mainly because of its popularity among other high schools in the area. He happily shared the good news with his friends and others that wished to listen. They generously congratulated him and wished that they too could be blessed with such opportunity. They regarded him as being so fortunate.

Chibuogwum's parents had got everything ready for his departure to Echianu High School for his secondary school education. Echianu High school was a boarding school. This meant that Chibuogwum would be away from his home and from his parents. Mr. Okereke, Chibuogwum's father had already bought all the things that Chibuogwum would need in the school, such as study materials like text books and exercise books, food and tea provisions.

The day for Chibuogwum to leave home and go to Echianu High school for his secondary school education arrived. They were to leave very early in the morning in order to get to the school on time, which was located about five hundred kilometres away from where they lived. It would take them about four hours or so to get to Echianu High school from where they resided. That early morning, as the light was yet on because the sitting room was still dark as the new day had not totally dawned, Chibuogwum's parents and Chibuogwum sat down in the sitting room. They wanted to give him some words of advice prior to his departure to school.

"My son, we are so happy and proud to have you as our son," Mr. Okereke began. "You have always been well-behaved. You have never disappointed us, not even once. But as you know, you are going to be away from us. You are going to be in an environment where our watchful eyes and parental training may not reach you on regular basis. We are aware that this may have some effects on you somehow. But if you continue to abide by what we taught you, you will by no means deviate from the road to life and righteousness that we have caused you to begin walking on. As we will not be there with you, the only way to succeed and avoid falling into evil is to avoid bad association. The place you are going to live is a place where you will meet different kinds of children from various backgrounds, different home trainings and mentalities. So, you must be careful in your choice of friends." Mr. Okereke paused. "I hope that you are hearing all that I am saying very well?"

"Yes, father, I am hearing everything you are advising me" Chibuogwum replied, "and I will do just as you have advised me."

Mr. Okereke nodded. "Very good. As I was saying, beware of bad friends who may influence you badly. Only choose good ones as your friends. Don't get involved in anything that will tarnish the good reputation of this family. Always be serious with your studies. If you have any problem there, let your teachers know about it without delay. If it is something that they cannot handle, they will know how to notify us. That's all I have to tell you. May God always be with you."

"Your father has really said it all," Uloaku began. "I am only adding that you should try to be obedient to your teachers and seniors in the school. Try also to apply all the advice you have been given by us today. I will not cease praying to God to continue to guide you, especially as you are going to be away from us. I will always commit you into God's hands. Always be a good boy. Don't disappoint this family."

Later, they left for Echianu High School in their private Sienna car with happiness. Mr. Okereke was the one driving, while his wife Uloaku sat beside him in the front seat. Chibuogwum sat at the back seat, relaxing well and reading a story book and sometimes watching outside from the car's window and enjoying the sights as the car moved on. But Mr Okereke and Uloaku chatted occasionally.

After more than four hours' driving, they got to the school gate and pulled up. It was indeed a magnificent edifice, with high fence and beautiful big gate. As they arrived at the gate, Mr.

Okereke sounded the car horn about three times. The gateman peeped from a small hole carefully constructed on the gate to see who it was before opening the gate. He opened the small gate and came out to have a better look at the car and to know who were inside it.

"Welcome, Sir. Welcome, Madam," the gateman greeted Mr. Okereke and his wife, bowing slightly.

"Good morning, my dear," Mr. Okereke and Uloaku replied simultaneously.

The gateman waved at Chibuogwum. "How are you, boy?" He smiled at Chibuogwum.

"I'm fine, sir. Good morning, sir," Chibuogwum responded.

The gateman returned inside the school compound through the small gate from which he had some out. Then, he opened the big gate and Mr. Okereke drove into the school compound. They enquired of the Principal's office. The gateman directed them. They drove straight to the Principal's office, parked their car at the front and walked into the Principal's office. They sat down.

"You are all welcomed," the Principal greeted Mr. Okereke and his wife, Uloaku.

"Good morning, Sir," Mr. Okereke and Uloaku reacted at the same time.

"Good morning, Sir, "Chibuogwum also greeted the Principal.

"Good morning, my son, "the Principal responded. "How are you?" The principal smiled at Chibuogwum.

"I'm fine, Sir," Chibuogwum replied and returned the smile.

"You may have seats," the Principal said, gesturing them to seats. They all lowered themselves to seats.

"We came to register our son. He was offered admission here for his secondary school education." Mr. Okereke began. "That is why we are here, principal."

"Fine. What's your name? The principal turned to Chibuogwum.

"My name is Chibuogwum Okereke," Chibuogwum answered.

"Date of birth?" the principal added

"14th August, 2011," Mr. Okereke replied.

"That's twelve years old." The principal remarked. "I hope that you are with his entrance result and admission letter?"

"Yes, Sir," Mr. Okereke answered. "Please, get them," he said to his wife, Uloaku.

Madam Uloaku brought out the entrance result and the admission letter from her pulse and handed them over to her husband, who in turn, gave them to the principal. The principal examined them and nodded with satisfaction.

"This is very excellent," the principal noted with joy. "He is very intelligent and brilliant."

"That's true, Sir, "Mr. Okereke replied contentedly.

"Your name and address? I hope you are his parents and sponsors?" the principal requested.

"Yes, Mr./Mrs Okereke Chijioke. Address is Ndioji Umuokwe."

"That's fine. Now, you will go to the next room and tidy up other thing there. There is a young woman there. She will direct you properly on what to do. Thank you immensely for coming." He handed them what he had written. "Give this to her when you get in." Chibuogwum and his parents left the principal's office and entered the next room where a young woman was sitting down behind a huge table with books on the table. They sat down.

"You are welcome," the young woman greeted politely.

"Good morning, Miss," replied Mr. Okereke.

"Good morning," Uloaku said.

"Good morning, Aunty," Chibuogwum greeted and slightly bowed.

"How are you, my boy?" she grinned at Chibuogwum.

"I'm fine, Aunty," Chibuogwum said.

Mr. Okereke handed her what the Principal had written. She examined it and nodded satisfactorily.

"That's very good," she observed. "I hope you know that this is a boarding school?"

"Yes, we are very much aware of that," Mr. Okereke replied in the affirmatives. "And I believe that with you people taking care of my son, he is in safe hands, both morally and otherwise."

"That's true. We take good care of children here. We endeavour to inculcate good morals into our students and ensure that they never at any time go astray. So, you can leave your son in our care without fear that he may deviate. We do our best to bring out the best in our students and ensure that they become useful to the society."

"I really appreciate that," said Mr. Okereke with a smile.

"Now, you are to pay his school fees, maintenance and other levies."

"All right. How much is it?"

"Everything is seventy-five Thousand eight hundred and fifty Naira (N75,850.00)."

"Do you accept transfer?"

"Yes, Sir,"

"Give me your account details."

The young woman wrote the school's account details on a piece of paper and handed over to Mr. Okereke. He brought out his mobile phone from his trousers' pocket and did the transfer which the young woman confirmed with thanks and nodding of the head.

"Thank you," the young woman acknowledged. "He has been assigned to dormitory B, room 48. We will give him all other things before two days, including school uniform, badge, constitution handbook. We will also conduct them round the school to enable them get to know all places in the school and be acquainted with the staff. Thank you so much for coming."

"Thank you too," Mr. Okereke responded. Then he said to Chibuogwum. "I will be leaving now. Chibuogwum, we love you so much. Try your best to be a good boy. Don't bring shame to us." He turned to the young woman. "Please, take proper care of him."

"I promise you that we will do our best."

Mr. Okereke and his wife Mrs. Uloaku departed. They entered their car and drove back home, happy that they had been able to get their son admitted into a prestigious boarding school where they hoped he would be given proper training.

CHAPTER TWO

F ew days later, Chibuogwum's maternal grandfather visited Okereke's house.

"I heard that my grandson did very well in her examinations" Mazi Chijioke began after sitting down. "I came to say congratulation to him. Where is he?"

"He has already gone to school," Mr. Okereke replied. "He got admission at a boarding school called Echianu High School. We took him there about four days ago."

"You mean that he is now a secondary school student at a boarding school?" Chijioke asked, amazed.

"Exactly," Mr. Okereke reacted.

"You mean he got admission, you got everything ready and took him to the school without even informing me? Is that good?"

"I'm so sorry about that, in-law," Mr. Okereke pleaded. "We were in a haste because we had a limited time, and we did not want to risk the admission being cancelled or terminated."

"Well, I am not complaining that I was not informed. I'm only worried over my grandson's welfare. I am also sceptical about the wisdom of this decision of yours to send your son to live in the school away from home and from your parental watchful eyes."

"You are right, father,". Okereke admitted.

"We carefully weighed that before we decided to do so. We advised him so well to always be of good behaviours and to also avoid bad friends who may badly influence him. We advised him to be respectful of his seniors and teachers and to take his studies very seriously. The school also pledged to do their best for him."

"Nevertheless, it is still your duty to be with your children and train them properly as their father," Chijioke noted. "Nobody can care for a child like his or her own parents.So, I feel that the decision you took to send him out to a boarding school, is not in his own interest. It is not a wise choice either."

"Well, I believe that with God's help, everything will progress for our very good. All that you have said is fine. However, my hope is that God will guide and guard him," said. Okereke. "All we need to do is to pray to God to guide him well in the way of uprightness and continue doing so."

"That is true," Chijioke agreed. "But practical wisdom is still necessary. We must try and do our very responsibility. We should not see avoidable mistakes and yet make them. I am very much afraid that the boarding school you have sent Chibuogwum to may get him corrupted if we are not careful. So, as your father who is older than you are and more experienced too, I advise you to withdraw him from the school now that it is not yet too late."

"Father, to tell you the truth, this maybe so difficult to be done," Mr. Okereke Observed. "We have already spent huge amount of money on that. And as you know very well, things are not easy these days. I paid close to Eighty Thousand Naira for his school fees, including other things I paid for. It is not easy at all to risk forfeiting such a considerable sum of money. So, I feel that he should continue, considering what I've invested in it aalready."

"How much you have spent does not matter. What matters is how your son's future will be affected. I am still of the opinion that you should forget about what you have spent already and withdraw him from the school. I am not in support of him living in a boarding school. I am afraid that he will be badly influenced by bad associates."

Okereke appeared confused. "in-law, to tell you the truth, I know that your point is true. But I am really confused. I don't know what to do actually. I will always ask God to guide him there."

"Well, I have spoken my mind to you on the issue," Chijioke said. "I will always join you in praying God for his good. But I still believe that practical wisdom still needs to be applied in order to forestall and avoid future regret. He still needs constant parental discipline in order to remain unblemished."

They kept discussing the matter for a long time, Chijioke yet expressing his fear that Chibuogwum might be misled there in the boarding school. They both said that they would always pray to God not to let Chibuogwum go astray. Chijioke was greatly disturbed at heart, and it showed in his behaviour and countenance. Okereke began to develop mixed feeling about the good judgment of the choice he had made sending his son, Chibuogwum to a boarding school, away from home. He began to understand that as a father, it was his sole and primary duty to pay close fatherly attention to his children. He realized that sending Chibuogwum away would mean that he had entrusted his God-given responsibility towards his child to others. Those to whom he had entrusted the care of his child might not be totally committed with their whole mind and soul to doing so as he would be himself. Nevertheless, there was nothing he could do, so he thought, mainly because he had already spent huge amount of money in his admission and therefore could not bear losing it by withdrawing Chibuogwum from the school, which his in-law, Chijioke had advised him to do. He resolved to leave everything pertaining to his son's future in God's hands.

Chijioke was still very much worried about Chibuogwum's safety there in the boarding school. After a long and deep thought, he decided to consult Odumodu, a renown dibia (priest doctor) to prepare something for him for Chibuog-wum's protection.

The priest doctor's shrine was uniquely decorated that it usually created certain effects on visitors – fear.

"My child, may it be fine with you," Odumodu said to Chijioke by way of response after the latter had narrated his worries to him as they sat facing each other. Odumodo often addressed each of his clients as 'my child' even if the person was older than he was. He was a short and robush man in his mid sixties. He painted his eyelids and wrists white, tied red and black cloth and tender palm frond round his head. He was bare, except for the gown he wore which ran utmost down his ankles. His ankles had anklets with little bells that jangled any time he stamped his feet on the ground or walked about. Odumodo sat on a tiger's skin which he had spread on the bare floor, while Chijioke sat on a small rough log opposite Odumodu.

"Your case is nothing to me," Odumodo said in a tone of confidence in his ability in his profession and authority. "I will do my best for you as a powerful priest doctor to make sure that his safety is guaranteed anywhere he may be. I'm an honest spiritual man. If I can't do something that a client of mine asks, I will be truthful and tell the person that I will not be able to do it. As I have told you, I can handle your problem and solve it."

"I will be more that elated if you help me with this problem of mine," Chijioke pleaded meekly and desperately.

Odumodu muttered incomprehensible incantation. Then he said.

"We will have to make sacrifices to the gods on your grand-child's behalf. You are to bring three full grown he – goats, ten mature cocks, five bottles of hot drinks, twenty tubers of yam, two baskets of kola nuts, four jars of palm wine and a litre of honey. Once you provide those things, I will sacrifice to the gods on his behalf and all will be with him anywhere he is," Odumodo explained.

"Ok. I will try to provide those things in two weeks' time," Chijioke promised. I will leave now."

"Once you do that, everything will be fine," Odumodo assured him.

Chijioke left.

CHAPTER THREE

F ew days after Chibuogwum was admitted into Echianu High School, the newly accepted students assembled to be addressed by the school principal. He stood before the newly admitted students, numbering more than one hundred and fifty.

"I, my vice and teachers are so glad to welcome you all to Echianu High School. As you all know, Echianu High School is a very popular school and has been in a leading position since its establishment over fifty years ago. Echianu High School produces seasoned and intelligent students who can do excellently in anything they are engaged and compete with other students anywhere. We ensure that we inculcate good morals in our students, that they are well disciplined and hardworking in all that they do," the principal said, addressing the students, "The reason you are here is to be trained to become useful to yourselves, your parents and society at large so that you justify all that your parents invest in your education, proving that they are not a waste. Therefore, I advise you all to focus completely on your studies and stay clear from anything that may distract you from what you are here for. You are very well aware that

Echianu High School is a boarding school and does not tolerate rubbish, especially loitering. So, we are very strict in enforcing our rules and regulations and in punishing defaulters. Your parents sent you here and entrusted to us the responsibility of caring for you. We must do our very best to prove that the trust and confidence they repose in us is not a mistake." He paused. "So, we must not hesitate to punish any of you who breaks any of the laws we have outlined in the handbook you've been given. If we fail in our duty to train you properly, the blame will be ours. That is why we should put our best effort to ensure that you are well trained.

"After this speech of mine, you will be conducted round the school premises to get acquainted with the compound and all in it. I and my Vice, Mr. Nwankwo and a few other teachers will do that. Then, tomorrow, your class lessons will commence in full. Once again, I exhort you to be good children and make sure that you don't default any of the school laws given to you. Thank you all. I wish you all success as you stay in this school and after," the principal concluded.

The newly admitted students were later conducted round the school. Each of the teachers also introduced himself or herself to the students and the subject he or she taught. The students were elated to be welcomed to the school which popularity had spread everywhere, far and near, and which every child longed and dreamed to attend. Chibuogwum was no exception. He was happy to be among the newly admitted students.

Later after the exercise of conducting them round the school compound, Chibuogwum was approached by a fellow student as he sat alone at the front of their classroom.

"Hello! My name is Chika. I am happy to meet you," the boy said. "May I sit beside you and let's talk?"

"Why not? You are free to do so," Chibuogwum replied.

Chika sat down with Chibuogwum. "As I have said, my name is Chika – Chika Maduka. May I know your own name?"

"My name is Chibuogwum, Chibuogwum Okereke," Chibuogwum answered.

"I guess you are one of the newly admitted students. Am I correct?"

"Yes," Chibuogwum said.

"I have been in this school for more than a year now. I am in Jss2. I was admitted about this time last year. I saw you and took keen interest in you. I know that it is not easy to cope in a school as this, with endless rules and restrictions, especially for new ones like you. However, with my help, you can avoid all that and enjoy your stay here with the right people."

"I don't understand your point," Chibuogwum noted with perplexity. "Is this place a difficult place to stay? This is a very good place to be."

Chika laughed. "That is because you have not started seeing the real side of the school way. Very soon, you will begin to understand what I mean. But I will always be available to help you if you permit me, as I have take interest in you. I want us to be close friends, so that we can be of help to each other."

"Yes, we can be..." Chibuogwum stopped suddenly. He remembered that his parents had warned him against having bad friends so that he would not be wrongly influenced. Half of his mind told him that this boy that wanted him to be his friend may be amongst such ones that his father and his mother had warned him not to form any friendship with. But the other part of his mind cast that thought aside, telling him that the boy was good and meant well for him and truly wanted to help him. Nevertheless, Chibuogwum was afraid not to disobey his parents, thus displeasing them and risking spoiling his future. So, he resolved that he must be careful in his choice of friends, and highly selective too.

"What's the problem?" Chika asked as Chibuogwum stopped abruptly and did not complete what he was saying. "Is anything wrong? Go ahead and complete your statement."

"Nothing. I just remembered that my parents warned me to be wary of the type of friends I keep to avoid spoiling my good manner, destroy my future and soil my image. That is why I feel that I have to know you well before accepting to be your friend. I don't want to defy the order given to me by my parents who care for me and want my good."

"I understand how you feel," Chika said. "It is fine to listen to one's parents and obey them. I want to assure you that I will be a good friend to you. I mean good for you and wish to help you because I know how things are in this school for juniors, especially the new ones like you. You will never understand what I'm saying to you until you start experiencing it yourself."

"But you can explain it to me," Chibuogwum requested.

"You see, senior students in this school always treat juniors ones badly. They relish seeing junior ones shedding tears. To avoid that, you need to make friends with some of them so that you will always be defended."

"You mean that the senior ones here treat the junior ones badly here at will?"

"Exactly. They can frame any offence that the junior students commit and flog them, any time they want," Chika explained.

"That's terrible and unjust," Chibuogwum noted.

"That is school life. That's how it is. I suffered greatly in the hands of the senior ones here when I was newly admitted over a year ago. But someone pointed the way out to me. And I said that I too will do same for another person. That's why I told you about it in advance and to help you as much as I can," Chika declared.

"Why would they punish one who has not done any wrong?"

"That's what they do. And it is terrible," Chika reacted. "That is the reason I want to help you by pointing the way out to you."

At this juncture, an SS2 student approached.

"What are you both doing here at this time?" He demanded, trying to sound official.

"Nothing," Chika and Chibuogwum replied.

"Nothing?" Ikenna, the senior said, and added. "Kneel down, two of you."

Chibuogwum and Chika complied.

After some time, he told Chika to stand up.

"You can stand up and go, Chika." Chika stood up to go. Chibuogwum too tried to stand up and leave with Chika.

Senior Ikenna spoke harshly to him. "You, what are you trying to do?" he demanded.

"Sorry, senior," Chibuogwum pleaded. "But I thought you asked us to go."

"Shut your mouth and kneel down there." He hit Chibuogwum gently on the head with a stick he was holding. "Are you Chika?"

Chibuogwum obeyed and remained in his kneeling position. At this moment, Chibuogwum's heart started pounding in expectation of what might follow next. He remembered what Chika had told him just a moment earlier about how junior ones were badly treated by the seniors. Now, he had begun experiencing it himself. He began to wonder if this was what he was going to bear all the years that he would stay in the school and if he could cope successfully at all. He started to understand the reality of what Chika told him not so long before. He looked around him for Chika but only saw that he was gone, having been set free, leaving him alone to suffer in the hands of the senior all alone.

"Stand up," senior Ikenna commanded seriously and formally, trying to sound threatening.

Chibuogwum got up and started to go away.

"Where are you going to?" Ikenna demanded. "Will you come back here? Did I ask you to go? Chibuogwum complied immediately.

"Follow me!" senior Ikenna commented as he started going away.

Chibuogwum humbly obeyed and followed him behind as he led the way.

Ikenna led Chibuogwum to an uncompleted building. They entered. There were three other SS2 students already there. The sight of these three other SS2 students sent tremendous fear into Chibuogwum's heart, and veins. Senior Ikenna joined them as they stood in line. They instructed Chibuogwum to stand before them.

Out of fear, Chibuogwum obeyed instantly and stood right before the four seniors, quivering with fear. He began to sweat profusely, worried about what might occur next. His heart pounded so fast and loud that he could hear clearly the sound of his heart beat and wondered too if the others could hear it as well. As he stood before the seniors, they intently fixed gaze at him and regarded him with a mixture of pity and contempt. He stood there in their front for about five minutes in utter silence. Then, Ikenna ordered him in what sounded like mild tone:

"Kneel down," Ikenna ordered, pointing to the ground where Chibuogwum stood. Chibuogwum obeyed at once and went on his knees.

"Now, we are going to give you an assignment," another senior said. "Did you hear what I said?" He bent towards Chibuogwum.

Chibuogwum nodded.

"Can't you talk?" the senior required menacingly.

"Yes, I can talk. I heard what you said," Chibuogwum said as he nodded emphatically a few times. His eyes gradually began to turn red and to be filled with tears.

"Good," the senior remarked and nodded gently. "Now, your assignment is to sing the anthem of the angels."

Chibuogwum was puzzled. He had never heard of such anthem. How could humans with flesh and blood know the anthem of the angels who are spirits and live in the heavens above? He was immensely astonished. He wondered. He fearfully gazed at the seniors in utter confusion.

"Didn't you hear what he said?" Ikenna shouted at Chibuogwum. He repeated the question, now rephrasing it. "Did you hear what he said at all?"

There was a little period of silence, during which Chibuogwum uttered no words due to the fear that gripped his heart. His mind told him that he was in real trouble. Then, he replied.

"I heard what you said, but I don't know how to sing it," he managed to say in total apprehension. "I have never heard of such anthem before."

Ikenna and the other three laughed mirthlessly, holding Chibuogwum in ridicule. Ikenna moved about Chibuogwum, looking at him mockingly and disdainfully and waving the cane he was holding as if he was thinking of what to do next as punishment to Chibuogwum in substitution for the anthem of the angels. After some time, he spoke.

"Very well then," Ikenna intoned. "Since you don't know the anthem of the angels and therefore can't sing it, you have an alternative. That alternative is that you should move round this room twenty times on your knees." Ikenna stopped moving and stood one place looking Chibuogwum all over with a display of an authority as senior.

Move around the room twenty times on his knee? Chibuogwum was shocked to his very marrow. How could he endure the pains that would result from moving about the room on his knees for a whole twenty times and the bruises he might sustain? He stared wildly in alarm.

"Please, seniors, be merciful to me." He burbled.

"What do you mean?" Ikenna yelled at Chibuogwum and raised the cane he was holding with his whole strength, and it landed heavily on Chibuogwum's back. Chibuogwum screamed. His screaming could pierce the heart. He clutched the spot on his body on which the cane had landed. Tears began flowing from his eyes. The senior hushed him up as they threatened him.

"If I hear your voice again, you will be sorry for yourself," Ikenna barked at Chibuogwum.

"Now, start moving round the room on your knees. Don't be silly?" he blared peremptorily.

Chibuogwum was immediately forced into silence. He started crawling round the room on his knees.

CHAPTER FOUR

Okereke sat in the sitting room after the discussion with his father in-law pondering over what they talked about Chibuogwum as he thought deeply and reflected upon the past, he recalled how he had been able to marry Uloaku after overcoming great obstacles. Years back, he had gone to the city and lived for many years. Later, he came back to his village Umuaku with a young woman and showed her to his mother, Ngozi and also told her that it was she that he wanted to marry. The young woman's name was Uloaku. Uloaku was not a native of Umuaku, the hometown of Okereke. But she hailed from another village called Amanri. He remembered all that had happened and the condition that surrounded Chibuogwum's birth as he slumped into the sofa.

After Okereke showed Uloaku to his mother and told her that it was she he wanted to marry as his wife, Ngozi refused to accept Uloaku as her daughter-in-law, saying that her son must never marry a person from other place other than Umuaku. Ngozi told Okereke to tell Uloaku that she was not interested in her being her son's wife. She also told him that the people of Amanri were not good, but bad people.

Okereke refused to accede to his mother's request, insisting on marrying Uloaku because he loved her so much. He said that Uloaku was beautiful, wise, intelligent and understanding.

Ngozi later consulted her bosom friend, Uchechi and told her that Okereke wanted to marry from Amanri. She went on to tell Uchechi that she had already warned Okereke her son not to marry the young woman. Uchechi commended Ngozi for her actions and advice to Okereke so far. She told Ngozi that she had some help to offer her if Okereke refused to leave the young woman.

Ngozi begged Uchechi to tell her what to do to make sure that Okereke never married Uloaku. Uchechi told her about a certain warlock called Okoronkwo. Uchechi told Ngozi that the man was powerful and could do nearly all things. Ngozi then asked Uchechi what she thought the warlock could do for her to help her in her condition and when they should visit him. Uchechi replied to Ngozi that the spiritualist would do anything that she would ask him to do for her to ensure that Okereke did not marry Uloaku. She told Ngozi that any time she was ready, she would be glad to take her to the man.

Three days later, Uchechi took Ngozi to the medicine man's place. Okoronkwo prepared a charm for Ngozi to make Uloaku unable to conceive and bear a child. He told Ngozi that he had found out that Okereke loved Uloaku so much and that there was nothing he could do to separate them or make Okereke to stop loving her. He said that the only thing he could do was to seal Uloaku's womb, which would force Okereke to send her out of his home if she stayed for years without a child. Okoronkwo warned Ngozi that any day Uloaku that conceived and bore a child, she would go blind.

They thanked Okoronkwo so much and departed. Optimistically, Ngozi waited for the outcome of her visit to the medicine man. She had offered the sacrifice, and was now waiting to see if the spirits would be found guilty.

Later on, Okereke returned to the city with Uloaku. Okereke went and properly married Uloaku in accordance with the customs of Amanri people, despite efforts from her mother, Ngozi, to dissuade him from marrying Uloaku. Ngozi was unhappy that Okereke disobeyed her and went ahead to marry a woman that she advised him not marry. Okereke and Uloaku lived for eight years, but they had no child.

Ngozi thought that Uloaku's bareness would cause Okereke to send her away. But that did not happen. Rather, Okereke continued to love her so much. Ngozi then resorted to accusing Uloaku of bewitching Okereke so that Okereke would not know what he was doing and only do her biddings.

One day, Ngozi went from Umuaku to the city where Okereke and Uloaku took residence. When she entered the house, Uloaku greeted her. Instead of responding to Uloaku's greeting, she asked her where her children were.

Uloaku told her that she was yet childless. Ngozi asked her why. Uloaku replied to her that she was not God who gives children, that she was waiting God's time, for God's time was the best.

Ngozi began to abuse Uloaku, calling her a wicked person because she wanted her to die without seeing her grandchildren. Then, she went on to threaten Uloaku that she must bear a child or else pack out of her son's house. Ngozi called Uloaku a man and said that Okereke her son married a fellow man without knowing it, thinking that he married a woman. Our people say that he who abuses a poor person abuses his God. Uloaku started crying, calling on God to help her shame the devil. She told Ngozi that what she was doing to her was not good.

Ngozi shouted at her to shut her mouth, that the way she was acting was how evil people behaved. She told Uloaku that she was a heartless witch. Ngozi said in her mind that if Okereke returned in the evening, she would make him to understand that she was not happy that she had not had a grandchild; that she would tell him things that would move him to send Uloaku packing and marry another woman.

Ngozi later carried out her thought. She called Okereke and started weeping and sobbing, saying that it hurt her so much at heart that she was yet to have a grandchild from Okereke. With tears of deceit, she told Okereke to divorce Uloaku and marry another wife. She told Okereke that if he wanted her to remain alive, he must do what she said.

Okereke declined to do what his mother, Ngozi said. He let his mother know that he was willing to wait until God gave them their own child. Okereke told Ngozi about some people told about in the Bible who were once childless but were later blessed with the fruits of the womb by God, like Hannah, Sarah and Elizabeth. He also said that he had strong hope that the same God who blessed those people with children of their own, would give them their own child in His due time.

Ngozi hissed and said that she was not interested in those meaningless stories; that what she needed was Uloaku to bear her grandchildren or Okereke should marry another woman who could give him a child. Ngozi said that if Okereke refused to send Uloaku out, that she would be maltreating Uloaku until she would be forced to run out of her son's home.

Okereke told his mother that he had already married Uloaku and that nothing would make Uloaku leave his house or stop being his wife. He told Ngozi that she was only troubling herself, thinking that she was tormenting Uloaku. Our people say that the grasshopper being burnt by the fire thinks that he is emitting oil. Okereke let his mother know that she was only wasting her time.

Ngozi later reported the issue to her husband's brothers so that they could help her, for our people say that when many persons jointly urinate at same spot, it foams. Ngozi's brothers-in-law sent message across to Okereke to come home and see them. Their message got alright to him, and he returned home without delay, although he could not guess why they sent for him.

Okereke and his uncles gathered. They were three, including Okereke and Ngozi, making them five persons. They began to speak to him seriously, saying that they were unhappy that Uloaku had not been able to bear a child for him. They said that such a condition is bad, for it might lead to the closure of his lineage and loss of his name if he died. They advised him to divorce Uloaku and get another wife who could bear him a child so that his lineage would not be discontinued after he had passed away, and for the continuation of his father's name.

Okereke told them that he would neither marry another wife nor send Uloaku away. They told him that there was no problem if he did not want to send out Uloaku. They said to him that he could marry another wife in addition to Uloaku, in order to have a child that would bear his name. However, he told them that he didn't want to marry two women and that he would never divorce Uloaku.

After Okereke said that, Ngozi threw herself to the ground and started crying, saying that Okereke her son wanted her to die when it was not yet her time. She lamented that all her mates have had grandchildren except her. She wept and told Okereke that all those born at the same time he was born have had three or four children of their own, while he was still childless. She began asking God why He allowed such evil to befall her. Ngozi cried and rolled herself on the ground, asking Okereke why he had refused to heed the good advice of her mother and uncles but chose to do what would bring him trouble and regret at last.

Okereke attempted to console Ngozi his mother. He told her that he had done nothing evil, but that he must exercise patience and wait until it was the will of God to give them their own child. Okereke said he would never do what he knew was bad.

Okereke's uncles spoke for more than two hours, trying to win Okereke over. But their efforts yielded nothing, for Ok-ereke was determined to continue to marry Uloaku, no matter anything. They tried in vain to make Okereke change his mind. Everything was just like pouring water on ducks. At last, they all dispersed.

Ngozi knew why Uloaku, Okereke's wife was childless. It was merely due to hatred simply because Uloaku did not come from Umuaku that she got her bewitched and sealed her womb so that Okereke could send her out. Although she was able to render Uloaku childless, her intention that Okereke would send Uloaku away, was futile. As a result, she started to devise other ways to treat Uloaku badly to force her out of her son's home, so that her son could get another wife, somebody from Umuaku. Ngozi devised an evil plan in her heart in order to continue causing Uloaku more sorrow, so that she would find it difficult to endure and then leave her son's house.

One day, Okereke came to Umuaku, their hometown to see her mother, Ngozi, to know how she was faring. Ngozi told him that she no longer wanted to live at Umuaku but that she wanted to come to the city and live with them. She wanted to go and live with them in order to be close to Uloaku so as to intensify her maltreatment of Uloaku to make her run away from her matrimonial home since Okereke had refused to send her out and marry another woman.

She said that her goal would best be actualized if she lived with Okereke and Uloaku , for the safest place to hold a bull is at horns. Okereke and Uloaku were yet to see real trouble from Ngozi. Her present actions were only a preamble of the real troubles from her. Our people say: Do not drink palm wine from raffia palm trees for palm wine produced from the real palm trees is still coming.

Ngozi later packed her things and moved to the city to live with Okereke and Uloaku. Okereke was not at home when she arrived, only Uloaku was in the house. Immediately Uloaku saw Ngozi, she rushed to her, greeted her and tried to collect her bags from her and take them inside. Sadly, Ngozi refused to respond to Uloaku's greeting or let her take her luggage in. Ngozi harshly said to Uloaku that greeting her and carrying her luggage inside were not her needs, that her major need was for her to bear a grandchild for her. Ngozi shoved Uloaku out of her way, telling her to make a way for her to pass. Uloaku almost fell down.

In tears, Uloaku asked Ngozi the reason she was treating her badly. She also told her to be aware that God knew everything and that God would pay everyone according to his or her deeds, and therefore should be careful of how she was treating her.

Upon hearing that, Ngozi's rage flared up. She shouted and raved and called Uloaku a man and told her to get out. She screamed at her that the only thing she knew was to stay at home and eat, not knowing that the most important thing was to bear children for them.

The following day, Uloaku was in the sitting room watching television when Ngozi entered and switched it off, saying that watching television was not the proper thing Uloaku should be doing, but that she should be bearing children. Not only eating and watching television for free. Ngozi said that one who did not know how much a hoe costs, uses it recklessly and carelessly. She ordered Uloaku out of the sitting room. But Uloaku wouldn't comply. Angrily, Ngozi went to where Uloaku sat down and pulled her up, trying to drag her into her room.

At this juncture, Okereke's voice was heard as he was coming back home. On hearing his voice, Ngozi threw herself to the ground and started crying and writhing as if in pains. Okereke entered and saw his mother rolling herself on the floor and writhing and asked what happened. Before Uloaku could open her mouth to narrate what happened, Ngozi had already started talking. Ngozi told Okereke that as Uloaku was in the sitting room watching television, she entered and joined her but that Uloaku told her to go away from the palour because she was an old woman, that old women shouldn't be watching television. She told Okereke that when she wanted to ask Uloaku what she did to her, she pushed her down.

Uloaku started crying and said that her mother-in-law lied against her. Then, she related the whole incident. But Ngozi insisted that Uloaku lied. Plainly, Okereke told Ngozi that the way she was treating Uloaku his wife only because she was yet to bear them a child was not just. He then switched on the television and told Uloaku and Ngozi to forget everything that happened and continue watching the television together, without any of them disturbing each other.

Ngozi said that Okereke should have vehemently rebuked Uloaku. She told Okereke that the reason he was taking sides with Uloaku regardless of her evils was that Uloaku had bewitched him. She slapped the top of the table and said she must show Uloaku the type of a person she was. She got up in anger and entered her room.

Our people say that when an animal needs to scratch on its body, it goes to a tree, but humans go to fellow humans when such needs arise. As a result, Uloaku travelled down to her home town to report her plights to her parents.

The first person to speak after hearing her story was her father, Chijioke. He told her that they had heard her report. He also told her that matters of such kind were temptations which she should be very careful of. Then, he told her that her mother would be in a better position to address the issue, for it was a feminine matter. Because the rope knows the parcel and the parcel knows who tied it; and also because to know what happens in the land of the spirits, it is better to ask owl or rodent.

Obidiya, Uloaku's mother began her talk with Uloaku by consoling her for all that she was experiencing at her matrimonial home. She told her that many married women also passed through similar conditions at their husbands' places, either from their husbands' parents or the relations of their husbands. She said that all she needed to do was to be patient and always pray for God's help, so that her mother-in-law would change her mind towards her.

Uloaku told her mother that she never offended her mother-in-law and that she had been so nice to her in order to make her happy. But all her efforts were in vain. Tearfully, Uloaku told her mother that she felt it was better to leave Okereke so that she could have rest of mind. She said that it was better for her to start looking for the black goat now that there was still light of the day before night came when there would be darkness. She also said that since those with whom she was hunting a spirit have turned to her and said that her head looked as a spirit's, it was better to join spirits and hunt for humans, because if she continued to be with humans, they would do to her what they planned to do to the spirit.

Obidiya told her to calm down and be hopeful that one day things would get better. She also told her that love is patient, especially in times of troubles, which she found herself in. Obidiya explained to Uloaku that if she loved Okereke her husband really, she should not let anything ruin her love for him, not even the present situation. But that she should continued to show endurance and keep praying to God for help. She told her that since Okereke still loved her despite pressures from his mother and relations, that was the most important thing. Obidiya greatly comforted Uloaku her daughter and told her many things that could be of help in her situation. She assured her that one day, things would be normalized.

Uloaku actually got true comfort from her parents. She thanked them immensely for their words of advice and comfort. They in turn, extolled her for reporting her problem to them, which showed that she trusted them. Uloaku later returned to her matrimonial place.

Immediately she got home, she began to apply her parents' advice. Nevertheless, the troubles from her mother-in-law intensified. Ngozi continued to treat her badly in various ways. As Obidiya advised her, Uloaku kept exercising patience to her mother-in-law and being good to her as best she could, despite Ngozi's opposition and maltreatment. She avoided anything that could make people say that she was ill treating her mother-in-law and she kept praying to God daily.

Ngozi's ill treatment of Uloaku worried Okereke greatly. As a result, he always spoke to her soothingly, comforting her. Okereke always told Uloaku to concentrate on him, and not on his mother and all her evil acts against her. He promised her solemnly that he would never cease loving her and that nothing would make her stop being his wife, in spite of all persuasions from his mother and his other relatives.

All of Okereke's words really touched Uloaku's heart and brought her inner peace and tranquillity. For this reason, she continued to staywith Okereke regardless of her mother-in-law's ill-treatment.

On her own part, Ngozi was determined that she must never allow Uloaku have rest of mind. She kept tormenting her in many ways in order to provoke her to anger. She began spreading false rumour that the reason Uloaku had not been able to bear a child was because she was a witch and that she used her witchcraft to eat her unborn children. She disturbed her at home every day. However, Uloaku kept enduring all those things and asking God for deliverance from her plights and bring shame to the devil.

Time and again, Okereke told his mother that Uloaku must continue to be his wife, because it was his right and duty to choose whom to marry, not another person. He always pleaded with her to stop giving them troubles. Sadly, none of these yielded the expected result. Rather, Ngozi went on to treat Uloaku badly. She resolved to keep maltreating Uloaku until she could no longer stand it and leave her son's house by force.

One day as Uloaku was in the kitchen cooking, Ngozi entered and ordered her to stop the cooking. She accused her of putting evil medicine in the foods she served Okereke with, which always made Okereke to lose himself and misbehave. Ngozi said that thenceforth, she would be preparing Okereke's meal herself so that her son would not continue to eat food that contained evil medicine. Uloaku abandoned everything for her and left the kitchen.

When Okereke returned, instead of his wife Uloaku, Ngozi her mother brought his food for him. Therefore, Okereke guessed that something had gone abnormal. Okereke asked his mother why it was she that served him his food and not Uloaku his wife. Ngozi told him not to be bothered as she was the one to be cooking him food from then on, so that he won't keep eating the foods that Uloaku gave him which contained evil medicine to control him to her advantage.

Okereke grew hot with anger and refused to eat the food. He left the food. He plainly condemned her mother's actions to her very face. He told her that it was better that she went back to the village rather than staying with them and disturbing them.

Ngozi did all she could to make Uloaku leave Okereke's place, so that Okereke could marry another woman. But all her efforts failed. So, she began to think hard in order to figure out a way to force Uloaku out of her husband's house.

She consulted her friend, Uchechi again. This time, she told Uchechi that Okereke still loved Uloaku so much despite their efforts to destroy their love for each other. She let Uchechi know that Okereke still insisted on marrying Uloaku, in spite of her inability to bear him a child, which was the result of their diabolic acts against her. She went ahead and told her that what she wanted her to do for her was to take her to the medicine man's place again.

Uchechi asked Ngozi what she wanted Okoronkwo to do for her this time. She replied that she wanted him to make Uloaku run mad so that she would leave Okereke's house to enable Okereke marry another wife. Uchechi told her that there was no problem; that anytime she wanted to go, she was available to take her to the place. She also assured her that Okoronkwo was a strong and powerful medicine man and that he could do anything she wanted him to do for her. Ngozi thanked her so much and departed. It was at Umuaku that Ngozi came to meet with Uchechi her friend.

They agreed to consult Okoronkwo in four days' time. Ngozi said in her heart that she must do all she could to ensure that Uloaku was forced to leave Okereke' house, either in good or in bad; that she must not continue to allow Uloaku remain in her son's house.

On the fourth day, Ngozi and Uchechi travelled down to Okoronkwo's abode. They told him their reason for coming to see him. Ngozi explained to Okoronkwo that although he was able to render Uloaku childless, but that could not lead Okereke to divorce her. Rather, Okereke insisted on continuing to marry her. Ngozi pleaded with Okoronkwo to help her in this condition.

Okoronkwo asked her what she wanted him to do for her. Ngozi told him that she wanted him to make Uloaku run mad, since her bareness had not caused Okereke to send her away. She said that Okereke would never like to keep a mad woman as a wife. Okoronkwo accepted to do what Ngozi asked.

He told her how much to pay. Ngozi agreed and paid him without delay and Okoronkwo commenced his work. When he had finished what he was doing, he gave Ngozi a talisman in the form of a cross with a feather on the top and tied with black and red ropes all around. Okoronkwo told Ngozi to go home with it. He told her that immediately she got home, she should go into Uloaku's room when Uloaku was not in and wave it round the room four times while holding it in her hand. That she would witness something spectacular. He warned her never to allow water touch it. Okoronkwo told Ngozi that if water touched it, both this one and the previous charm would be rendered ineffective and that she would go blind and run mad.

Ngozi and Uchechi thanked him very well and left. Ngozi was overjoyed. But at the middle of their journey back home, the weather changed – the sky turned cloudy, wind followed. Presently, there came a very heavy rainfall. Ngozi did all she could to make sure that water did not touch the thing that Okoronkwo gave her, but all her efforts were of no use. The talisman got drenched. In fact, the rainfall of that day was nearly as that of Noah's day. Now, the God of the helpless was at work.

Instantly, Ngozi became blind and started acting insanely. Her friend, Uchechi abandoned her and fled. Ngozi kept wandering about and finally headed to an unknown destination, still blind. So, to be innocent is good.

Two months later, Uloaku got pregnant and delivered of a triplet nine months after – one male and three females. Indeed, they were very healthy and bouncing babies. Okereke and Uloaku named the first one Chibuogwum (which literally means "God is my medicine") and named the second one Chinagorom (which literally means "God is my vindicator") while they named the third one Chimamkpam (which literally means "God knows my needs".) The babies were so strong and good looking.

After, they invited people to join them and celebrate what God had done for them. Those that attended were as uncountable as the sand of the ground. Food, drinks and meat were in great abundance. Everything was in surplus. Musicians were on ground to entertain people and the people danced jubilantly to their very satisfaction and entertainment, because everyone was so glad. Everybody ate, drank and danced to his or her fill until late evening. Then, they left for their various homes one after another or in groups.

Truly, Uloaku and Okereke did not know how to thank God enough for all he had done for them. Of course, they could never have been able to thank him enough. They were filled with gratitude to God. It is exactly as our people say that the cow that has no tail, its god chases away flies for it. God is also the power and judge of the innocent one.

CHAPTER FIVE

Chibuogwum later narrated to his friend, Chika what he passed through in the hands of Ikenna and the other seniors. Chika felt pity for him and emphasized that that was the reason he should have a senior student as a friend for protection. For Chibuogwum, he had begun to learn that his survival and success in the school would largely depend on persistence and determination, that it was meant to be survival of the fittest. He decided that it would be useful to learn a trick or two from persons like Chika who have been in the school before him and who were ready to help, on how to cope successful, especially bullies from the senior students. He could now see vividly the discrepancy between primary school life where seniority was not an authority and secondary school life where seniority was viewed as an avenue to exhibit almost absolute power and authority over the Juniors. To his very utmost amazement, he saw with dismayal soul that the senior students seemed to derived relish from maltreating the junior ones.

As he sat alone at the front of their classroom during break period, the thought of what he passed through in the hands of Ikenna and the other seniors streamed his mind and incensed him greatly. It was not only his own experience that embittered his heart, those of his other fellow junior ones also did. He nearly regretted having applied to have his secondary school education in this boarding school called Echianu High school. However, he cast that feeling out of his mind and resolved to cope just as others were doing, no matter the challenge. He believed that anything he might experience in the boarding school, no matter how difficult it might be on him, would help in preparing him for similar future challenges. If he decided to withdraw from the school, his parents would certainly be unhappy, having paid huge sum of money for his admission. They won't even like to hear it, no matter what could be his reason for feeling that way, as those in the school were almost his peers.

Of course, they could not afford to forfeit all that they had spent on his admission just for what may seem to be no reason to them. Chibuogwum knew all this and resolved to remain in the school and endure, despite any challenge he might meet or encounter.

As he sat there in deep thought and totally engrossed in his feelings, he was approached by Chika and conversation ensued. Chibuogwum's face wore grim expression.

"How are you, Chibuogwum? Why are you not playing with others but alone?" Chika asked, looking at Chibuogwum.

"It's nothing," Chibuogwum replied coldly. "I don't want to play. I just want to stay alone."

Chika quickly detected that he was not in his normal self. "You look so cold and unlively this afternoon. What's wrong?"

"I'm not just feeling glad at all," Chibuogwum reacted.

"Is it because of the seniors? That is school life; that is what junior students pass through in the hands of senior students here. You will overcome it, only if you apply my advice. That is why it is necessary for you to get one of the seniors as your friend. He will be protecting you from maltreatment by the senior students."

"I have not told you what they did to me the day senior Ikenna took me away when I was with you. They maltreated me unkindly. I don't even have the mouth to narrate to you what I passed through in their hands that very day after we parted. What I experienced in their hands is very terrible and inexplicable. My ordeal in their hands ink me so much."

"I understand how you feel," Chika acknowledged sympathetically as he looked pitifully at Chibuogwum. "I had similar experience when I was newly admitted here. If I tell you my own experience, you will surely conclude that yours is fair compared to mine. It was indeed more than terrible." Chika shut his eyes tightly as he spoke by way of emphasis. "They are so merciless."

Chibuogwum shrugged. "It is so unbelievable, what they did to me." He frowned and his emotion began to soar slightly. "They did as much as asking me to crawl on a hard cemented floor on my bare knees. Just imagine such in human punishment, not on adults, but on children! It is so bad. My knees still pain me badly." He touched his knees and winked in pains.

"That is why I said that solution to this is to get a friend from among the seniors. Once you get one of them as a friend, all these will be over, just like I have experienced," Chika said confidently. "I know very well that it is not easy to cope here, especially for you new ones. I can attest to that."

"You are always talking about making one of them my friend. How can I do that?"

"That's a very nice question you have asked," Chika noted satisfactorily.

"I will talk to senior Ikenna about you. I'm sure he be willing to accept you as his young friend and will ever be ready to protect you, just as he does for me."

"Are you sure that he'll agree if you tell him about me?"

"Surely, he will," Chika assured Chibuogwum. "You know you are both handsome and intelligent too. So, he will be glad to have you as a friend of his. As I have said, I will talk to him about you."

"I believe that he will be a good fellow?" Chibuogwum asked, a little sceptical.

"He will," Chika assured him. "He is a nice person, but what matters most is the protection you are going to get from him, which every junior student in this school wants."

"If that is so," Chibuogwum said, "it is good. I will like to have him as a friend."

"Surely. You know very well that I can't mislead you. I know what happens in this school, that is why I told you everything the very first day I met you, because I took special interest on you as soon as I saw you," Chika explained. "All that I told you have all happened. Have they not?"

"They have," Chibuogwum affirmed.

"And that is why you should always trust me," Chika said convincingly.

At this moment, senior Ikenna approached them. The two boys kept silent as they looked at him.

"Good afternoon senior," they managed to utter at last.

"Good afternoon, Juniors," he replied. "How are you?"

"We are fine, senior," they answered simultaneously.

"So nice," Ikenna drawled. "Follow me, Chibuogwum," he said imperiously, pointing at Chibuogwum.

Chibuogwum complied reluctantly.

They entered uncompleted building. Ikenna climbed unto a window and sat. He removed his sandals and told Chibuog-wum to give his toes manicure service.

"Make sure that they are very nearly done. Did you hear?" He demanded.

"Yes, senior," Chibuogwum answered obediently.

Chibuogwum commenced rendering manicure treatment to Ikenna's toes, trimming and scrapping them. He remained at the service in silence for some minutes.

"You said your name is Chibuogwum?"

"Yes, senior," Chibuogwum replied.

"That's lovely," Ikenna intoned. "I guess you are one of the newly admitted students in JSS One?"

"Yes, senior."

"There's something I want you to know about. It is not easy to cope successfully in this school, especially in the hands of the seniors if you don't have one of them as your friend for protection." He paused. "I see you are a very nice boy who will make a fine junior friend. So, I have taken keen interest in you and I want us to become friends. If you become my friend, your protection is guaranteed. Do you accept to be my junior friend?"

"Yes, senior," Chibuogwum replied warmly.

"From today, we are special friends. Feel relax. If anyone dares touch you, whoever it is, let me know. With me, Ikenna the great python, you have nothing or anyone to be afraid of. Do you understand?"

"Yes, senior," Chibuogwum replied and nodded emphatically. "That's fine."

"That's good. I hope your parents are okay?"

"Yes, they are?" Chibuogwum replied.

"What's their occupation," Ikenna queried.

"They are into business," Chibuogwum said.

"I know that one day, you will be glad to know where I stay."

"Yes, senior, I will be more than overjoyed to know where you live," Chibuogwum said excitedly.

"That's nice, my boy," Ikenna said gleefully. "You see, you will still enjoy this our friendship. I will introduce you to my friends. They are real men of this school. With them and me, your protection is totally assured. They too will be your friends. Only be a good boy and comply to their terms. Did you understand?"

"Yes, senior," Chibuogwum replied and nodded affirmatively.

"In order to associate successfully with me and my friends and be our friend, you need to be smart and adventurous. I hope you get me well?"

"Yes, senior. I will try my best to fit in," Chibuogwum said.

Ikenna smiled mischievously. "I love your replies, my boy. I am beginning to sense that our friendship will work well."

Chibuogwum continued to treat Ikenna's toes and fingers. They remained silent for some minutes. Ikenna seemed to be enjoying the manicure treatment so much that he stretched out his legs to Chibuogwum and relaxed comfortably. Chibuogwum kept silent as he seemed to completely focused on the service-trimming and scrapping Ikenna's toes, fingers and thumbs. At last, Ikenna broke the silence.

"You seem to be an expert in this you are doing?" Ikenna jovially said in compliments.

Chibuogwum smiled satisfactorily. "Thank you. I don't even know that I am getting it done well," he said modestly. "I thought that I wasn't getting it well to your contentment."

Ikenna skillfully and deliberately changed the talk. "You say your parents are into business?" He asked, sounding somehow inquisitive.

"Yes, senior," Chibuogwum replied unsuspectingly.

"I hope they are well-to-do?" Ikenna probed on.

Chibuogwum replied unassumingly and cautiously too. "They have what is enough for us, at least our primary needs."

"That's so lovely to hear," Ikenna complimented.

"Thank you, senior," Chibuogwum acknowledged.

"How many are you in your family?" Ikenna enquired. He yawned.

"We are four, including my parents, making us six," Chibuogwum answered. "We are one boy and three girls. I am the first among the four of us."

"So you are the man of the house after your dad?" Ikenna smiled pleasantly at Chibuogwum. "You are the one to inherit your father's health as the first son, at least the greatest portion."

Chibuogwum chuckled. "Not yet. But when time for that comes, my siblings will all have shares."

"I can see that you have a kind heart," Ikenna declared. "Where did you do your primary school?"

"Diamond Primary School," Chibuogwum said.

"I know the school. It is a very good school," Ikenna commented. Silence.

"I'm through now", Chibuogwum announced and stroke his two palms together as if to remove dirt. He gave the razor blade he was using back to Ikenna. Ikenna examined his fingers and toes and was satisfied with what Chibuogwum had done to them.

"This is so wonderful," Ikenna praised. "I'm now more handsome than I was few minutes ago. You are wonderful."

Chibuogwum accepted his acclamation in silence. He was gradually beginning to feel relax with Ikenna and to enjoy the new friendship. He hoped it would continue that way, to his very happiness. With persons like Ikenna on his side, he had nothing to worry about in the school, he thought. He began to notice that all that Chika told him about Ikenna was true, at least at the moment. Ikenna and Chika, including their friends must be good fellows, he concluded in his mind. Ikenna jumped down from the window and slapped his buttocks a few times by way of dusting them.

"I will like you to visit my place by 06:30 p.m tomorrow. I live at Silver Dormitory, room 24," Ikenna said.

"Okay, senior. I will do so."

"Now, you may go."

As Chibuogwum was leaving, he met one of the senior students that had punished him earlier.

"Where are you from?" The senior demanded in an air of authority. Before Chibuogwum could open his mouth to reply, he added.

"Keep down and raise your hands."

Chibuogwum complied, without resistance.

Ikenna saw what was going on and called out to the other senior.

"No, senior. Leave him. He was with me," Ikenna explained.

"Is that so?" the other senior student asked rhetorically. Then, he said to Chibuogwum. "Get up and go."

Chibuogwum obeyed.

The other senior student walked up to Ikenna. "What were you doing with him?" He asked Ikenna.

"He is now my friend," Ikenna replied. He is a very nice boy. I hope to bring him into our group. I believe he'll be of immense use to us."

"I hope that he'll not betray us?"

"No. I have tested him. He is both smart and intelligent. All he needs is a little training. He can fit in."

"No problem, if you say so. I trust your choice."

CHAPTER SIX

T he weather was extremely cold. The sky was cloudy and hazy, making it difficult to see afar. It was the harmattan season, and the wind blew ceaselessly, throwing dry dust up and whirling leaves. The first rain of the year was about to fall, to revive or rejuvenate leaves that had withered in the face of the harsh harmattan. It was yet early morning and people were yet to spring into full activities of the day. The first rain of this very year was late in coming, unlike the past years'. The people had expected it to come about two months back or nearly. Each year, immediately after the first rain, the people usually started their farming works. They first cleared the bush and waited for some days for the hot sun that often emerged after the first rain to scorch the cut or cleared bush to dryness. Then they would set fire to it after separating the fire woods. Whatever that the fire did not consume would later be cleared or gathered together with rake or any other locally designed tool, such as sticks or hard brooms. After this, the land would be ready to be tilled and the soil made into mounds of various sizes, depending on the owner's choice.

Chijioke, Okereke's father-in-law and Chibuogwum's maternal grandfather sat at the front of his house in his hometown. He had already gone back after visiting his son-in-law, Okereke, during which he was told that Chibuogwum was in a boarding school for his secondary school education. He sat on a locally made bench, made of raffia palm bamboo poles and sticks with dual boughs. This type of local bench is made by staking two sticks of about two feet with two branches in the ground opposite each other with a space of around two feet or less in three different places and crossing beams on each of the three. Then, bamboo poles would be placed on the top. He was cleaning his teeth with a rough chewing stick and spitting out the pieces occasionally. He watched the weather and the darkened sky with happiness, for it indicated that it would soon rain.

He was among the few great and revered farmers in the community. His massive produce of yams had earned the little of little of Ezeji (King of yams) by the entire people of the village, celebrated in a colourful way. As he sat looking at the cloudy weather, his heart was filled with fathomless joy. As soon as it rained, he would begin his farming activities by first clearing the thick bush. Then he would next set fire to it when it had dried, clear the rubbish not consumed by the fire. After that, he would cultivate the soil into big mounds in which he would plant his yam seedlings, which had already started sprouting in his barn. He planned in his heart how he was going to engage in the year's farming works. He had planned to cover a large portion of land, because his yams had increased utmost double of the previous year. That very morning, he had scheduled to pay a visit to his bossom friend, Akubuike, whom he had not set eyes upon since his return from his in-laws' place. But now having seen the condition of the weather, he decided to wait.

A cock crowed loudly nearby, disturbing the quietness of the morning and nearly startled Chijioke. He attempted to hush it up by shouting at it. This stirred the other fowls nearby. They started shouting variously in alarm. Those at distant places heard them and joined in. Some people living nearby thought that they were being attacked by a predator, like a wild carnivorous animal.

Obidiya, Chijioke's wife emerged from the house and greeted him, adjusting her cloth which ran above her breasts, leaving her upper chest and shoulders bare. She stood beside her husband and scrutinized the weather for sometimes, as she folded her arms across her breasts and her hands under her armpits. She too regarded the weather with joy. The cloud nearly obscured the sky totally.

"Hmm," she grunted. "If it eventually rains, it will be very heavy. See how cloudy the weather is."

"That is true, mine," Chijioke concurred. "It is going to be a heavy rain indeed. "You know it's been long we began expecting the first rain of the year. It usually came before this time in passed years. Maybe it wants to give it all to us once today." He spat out pieces of chewing stick and looked at the sky as if examining it. It started rumbling. The cloud on the sky began to move to one direction.

"I pray that it doesn't destroy anything," Obidiya said. "I pray it doesn't come with heavy wind and destroy things as it did ten years ago. Let it rain peacefully."

"I also pray so," Chijioke agreed. "The rain of that very year was so terrible and destructive. It was so heavy that the torrent carried nearly all yams, and cocoyams planted in the farms that year. It rendered many great farmers poor and without yams and cocoyams with which to continue their farming. I thank God that I did not plant all my yams and cocoyams that very year but left some in the barn. If not, it would have surely been a different story altogether."

Obidiya shrugged. "It was truly so bad and unthinkable."

At this moment, Chijioke's bosom friend, Akubuike was seen approaching the house.

"Dry meat that fills the mouth," Akubuike hailed Chijioke as he came closer.

"One person that is welcomed as many." Chijioke returned the greeting.

"You are greater among the greatest ones," Akubuike eulogized.

"You are a mighty flood that carries rocks and logs," Chijioke saluted again.

Akubuike and Chijioke shook hands in a traditional fashion, like men with titles. They hit the backs of their hands against each other's gently, then shook hands properly. Akubuike sat beside Chijioke on the local bench, keeping his walking stick at his side.

"You are welcome, my good friend. It's been so long we met," Chijioke greeted. "I was planning to play you a visit today. I was wondering if you too travelled."

The rain started dropping sporadically, making sounds on the zinc roof. All of a sudden, the heaven was let lose. There came a very heavy downpour. The heavens murmured gently frequently and thunder boomed occasionally, loud and prolonged. The wind blew violently, causing trees to be twisted furiously from side to side. As the thunder roared, the sound echoed and reverberated on the roof, causing prolonged vibration. Lightnings came occurring continually, unrelenting. It rained heavily and drummed hard on the roof. The atmosphere kept roaring. Chijioke and Akubuike's voices were drowned almost completely that they talked at the top of their voices in order to hear each other.

The rain became heavier. Akubuike and Chijioke had to vacate the verandah and go inside as the wind kept splashing water towards the verandah. Torrents had already developed. Inside, it was semi-dark. Chijioke lighted the hurricane lamp.

"You are so lucky to have arrived before the rain began," Chijioke said to Akubuike.

"It seemed that it was waiting for me to come in," Akubuike said delightedly. A pause. "Like you asked before if I travelled, I did not travel. I decided that I would come and see you this morning before you go out, because it had been so long a time we saw."

"You did well. As I have said, I planned to visit you today," Chijioke proclaimed.

Chijioke rose and went into a room adjoining the palour. He returned with some lumps of kolanuts and hot drink in a tray. He deposited the tray that continued the kola nuts and the gin on the table.

"Here are kola nuts and drink," Chijioke announced. He sat down.

"I salute you, my great friend," Akubuike said, "For the kola nuts and drink you've brought. Our people say that he who brings kola nuts brings life."

"That is true," Chijioke confirmed.

Akubuike took one of the kola nuts and began to prepare it for prayer. First, he removed the coat. Then, he used his is nails to divide it. It was four lumps. With his nail, he extracted the eye of each. He gave them to Chijioke for prayer as the head and owner of the house in accordance with the tradition and culture of the Igbo people in Nigeria. In Igbo land, if there is a gathering of the kinsmen or friend's visit, it is the host who brings the kola nuts or drink that pours the libation and offer other traditional prayers, even if he is a small boy or the youngest among them all. He must be accorded that respect as the owner of the house. But if there are older men in the house, it is the right of the eldest among them to pray and pour libation. It is improper and unacceptable for a guest to pray or pour libation in The host's house in Igbo land, even if the visitor is much older than the host.

Chijioke collected the eyes of the kola nuts from Akubuike and stood up. He cleared his throat.

"Our ancestors," Chijioke commenced his prayer, "with this kolanut, we salute you. May our eating of this kolanut bring us good things."

"Iseeoo!" Akubuike replied.

"May what we'll plant this farming season flourish and yield abundantly."

"Iseeoo!"

"May the visitor not kill his host with his visit, and may he not go with a swollen back."

"Iseeoo!"

"May our wives bear us sons and daughters. And may we have things with which to train them."

"Iseeoo!"

"Let the kite perch and let the eagle perch. Any who says the other will not, may its wings be plucked out."

"May it be so," Akubuike chorused.

"May children bury their fathers, and not fathers their children. Protect us from premature and untimely death and other evils, and provide our individual needs,"

"Iseeoo!"

"Anyone who wishes his fellow evil, let him to be choked by his evils."

"So be it," Akubuike intoned.

Chijioke threw out the pieces of kolanuts at the front of the house and returned inside. Then, Akubuike poured some quantity of the hot drink into a small glass cup and handed it over to Chijioke. Chijioke accepted it, stood up and began to pray traditionally.

"Our ancestors, here I come again with hot drink. May good meet all of us. May we prosper in all that we do that is good."

"So be it," Akubuike affirmed.

"May good things come to our land and let evil things be chased away completely. Let goodness dwell and prevail among us."

"Iseeoo!"

"Let every evil plot be exposed and rendered powerless. Let all evil medicine in our land against anyone be made ineffective."

"Iseeoo!"

Chijioke poured some drops of the hot drink on the ground and drank what remained in the cup. Then, he returned to his seat.

The men began eating the kolanuts and drinking the hot drink.

"I welcome you from your visit to your son-in-law's place," Akubuike said. "I hope that it is well with them, especially your daughter and our daughter?"

"Yes, all of them are all right. It's just that I disapprove of a decision they made concerning my grandson, Chibuogwum."

"What did they do about him that you do not like?" Akubuike asked.

"They got him admitted in a boarding school, far from home."

"Ehe! What's wrong with that?" Akubuike asked rhetorically. "Living in a boarding. School will help him concentrate fully on his studies and avoid much plays and unnecessary games watch home students engage in. His admission into a boarding school will keep him under the watchful eyes of the teachers almost at all times, unlike children who come to school from home. So, I don't think that there is anything bad in their decision for your grandson to have his secondary school education at a boarding school. It's for his good, now and in future."

Chijioke was stunned. "Is that how you see it?" Chijioke asked. "Is that the only way you look at it? Have you not seen that some of the children sent to boarding schools got corrupted and brought to their parents disappointments and headaches. I fear and foresee that my grandchild might get corrupted."

"You should not wish them that. Even if others have experienced that, I pray that his will be among the successful ones. It is true that it is one God that creates, but it is not the same destiny that controls."

"That's true," Chijioke agreed. "But we must do the right thing at the right time, and let's not have the blame."

"Now, what do you intend to do about it?"

"I have already spoken my mind to my son-in-law about it. However, his worry is that he has paid a considerable amount of money for his admission, and he finds it difficult to withdraw him from the school, for it will mean losing all that he had spent there already. He asked that we always pray for his success and protection from negative influences," Chijioke expanded.

"That is what you and others should be doing," Akubuike said.

"I have already begun doing that," Chijioke said. "Not only that, I have also visited Odumodu for additional traditional help. And I believe that both my prayers and Odumodu's acts will yield the required result, or either of the two."

"Whatever is done, my confidence is that nothing shall come upon your grandchild wherever he is," Akubuike said confidently. "I pray he will go there, do his studies and return successful and triumphantly and make us proud."

"I pray so too," Chijioke agreed. "I'm deeply worried, that is why I am doing all I can to ensure that nothing evil will happen to him."

"Hmm," Akubuike sighed. "My prayer in all this is that he will excel in his studies and bring home the bacon. I pray that he'll be safe from all evil, including bad influence and come back here and increase our joy and pride in him. He is already an intelligent and a well-behaved child that we are proud of. My believe is that God will make his going there successful."

"Your wishes are good," Chijioke said.

The rain had subsided. The men sat quietly for some time. Akubuike crossed his legs in relaxation and creaked his teeth gently. He brought out his snuff container from his pocket and tapped lightly on it and opened it. He scooped some quantity with his thumb, guided it towards his nostrils and stuffed them plentifully with the snuff. He sneezed loudly and spontaneously and shed tears profusely. He closed the snuff container and cleaned his nostrils and cleared the tears that the intake of the snuff had caused to gush out.

CHAPTER SEVEN

C hibuogwum lied on his bed in his room. He was reflecting upon his newly started friendship with senior Ikenna.

"Oh, that senior Ikenna is a nice fellow and friendly too," Chibuogwum thought aloud. "I'm glad to have got him to be my friend. With him, I am sure that nobody will punish or torture me again in this school, because he is so popular and others obey his commands. He is capable of protecting me. I'm sure of that." He paused and rolled himself on the bed excitedly. "Oh, I have an appointment with him this evening in his hostel by 6:30. I must get ready immediately and start going."

He rose, got dressed up and set out for Ikenna's place. In less that ten minutes, he was in Ikenna's room.

"Welcome to my humble abode," Ikenna smiled at Chibuogwum. "Sit down." He pointed to a small wooden stool at the edge of his bed.

"Thank you, senior," Chibuogwum said, sitting.

"You just arrived at the right time. I have an important meeting with my friends tonight, at 08:30. I hope you will be happy to be part of it?" Senior Ikenna waited, expecting a reply from Chibuogwum.

Chibuogwum was silent for some moment.

"Come on, my boy. Stop hesitating," Ikenna urged. "You will surely like it. You will greatly enjoy it. There, I will formally introduced you to them. You are going to meet key and relevant students that this school has."

"Okay, senior. I will like to be there."

"Good. Are you going to wait here until then or do you want to go and come back?

"I will like to go and return."

"8;30 is the time. Don't forget," Senior Ikenna reminded him.

"I will not."

Chibuogwum returned to Ikenna's room at exactly 8:25 p. m.

"Let's start going. It's almost time others might have begun arriving."

Few minutes later, Chibuogwum and Ikenna arrived at the uncompleted building wherein they had punished Chibuog-wum. They entered. There was a dozen other students already there, all ruggedly and roughly dressed. At the middle of the room was a rickety wooden table on which are packets of ciga-rettes, assorted hot drinks, beers and lighter. They all sat round the table chattering pleasantly.

"Boss man!" "Leader." "Presido!" "Senior man." They hailed Ikenna variously as he entered with Chibuogwum.

He acknowledged the greeting by waving his hands.

What Chibuogwum saw amazed him to his very marrows. He was slightly terrified as all eyes were fixed on him, being an unknown person. Ikenna realized his ordeal and came to his rescue.

"Great dragons!" Ikenna saluted the gathering.

"Oneness!" they boomed simultaneously.

"Great dragons!" Ikenna saluted again.

"Unity of action!" they all responded.

"Great dragons!"

"Be your brother's keeper!"

"I welcome you all to this crucial meeting."

Before I go ahead with today's agenda, may I introduce to you a new member of this group. All of you have been looking at this boy that I came with surprisingly. He is my new junior friend, and he is here to join our group. I've tested him, and he is both smart and intelligent. His name is Chibuogwum. He is one of the newly admitted students in JSS One." He took Chibuogwum to the center.

Chibuogwum was dazed. His feet were almost trembling and nearly unable to carry his body. He was visibly frightened. He stood there at the middle as Ikenna returned to his position and continued to address the group.

"Great dragons!" he hailed.

"Oneness!" they responded.

"Great dragons!"

"Unity of action!"

"Great dragons!"

"Be your brother's keeper."

"I greet you all again," Ikenna said. "May we now welcome our new member official."

"Welcome to great dragons family,

A place of oneness.

Welcome to great dragons family,

A place of unity of actions,

Welcome to great dragons family,

Where we are our brother's keepers," they sang repeatedly as they moved round Chibuogwum in circular pattern.

After, they all settled down.

"Before we go into our agenda for today's meeting, let us first make ourselves happy," Ikenna said. "You can all enjoy yourselves with these things on the table."

They all started to drink and to smoke. Chibuogwum was transfixed and flabbergasted by what was going on. He sat timidly and watched the others in full astonishment as they drank and smoked. That was not what he had expected to see.

Ikenna filled a cup with beer and went and sat beside Chibuogwum.

"Take this and join us in the merriment," Ikenna said to Chibuogwum.

Chibuogwum was shy and afraid too.

"No, senior. I don't take alcohol. If I take it, I will get intoxicated," Chibuogwum whispered to Ikenna, gently resisting.

"There is nothing bad in it. Just take a sip, and you will certainly enjoy it," Ikenna persuaded. "In fact, once you've tasted it, you will like it and even ask for more,"

Chibuogwum remained calm and hesitant. The others started mocking him, as they saw that he was not yielding.

"He is still his mother's baby."

"Boy, are you still being breastfed?"

"Maybe he is a girl."

"He wants to return to his mother's womb."

"He is a she."

They all laughed derisively at Chibuogwum and looked at him disdainfully.

Out of shyness, Chibuogwum accepted the drink from Ikenna and sipped a few times. Then, he stopped. Ikenna urged him to have more. The others did likewise, praised and clapped for him. Chibuogwum sipped more.

"Now, you are getting it properly, boy," Ikenna commended. Next, Ikenna lighted a stick of cigarette and gave it to Chibuogwum. "Put it in your mouth and draw the smoke."

Chibuogwum collected the cigarette from Ikenna. Gently, he began to raise it towards his mouth.

The others looked on and hailed him.

Finally, he put it in his mouth and inhaled the smoke. He started coughing.

"Go on," senior Ikenna benignly urged Chibuogwum on. The others clapped for him and pressed him on.

"It's entered my brain,". Chibuogwum complained and shook his head vigorously. Tears started flowing out of his eyes.

They all laughed.

"You've got it," Ikenna said in praise to Chibuogwum. "Take more."

"It's scattering my brains. Let me rest a little," Chibuogwum gently protested.

Ikenna kept persuading and pestering him to take more. At least, he compromised.

He drew in more smoke, now improving.

"You are improving," Ikenna noted. "That is nice. Keep it up, my boy."

The others cheered.

"I told you that you would like it when you have tasted it," Ikenna said. "How do you see it? I hope it is good?"

Chibuogwum nodded.

"You are now a big boy, in fact, a real man," Ikenna said to Chibuogwum. "You are really going to enjoy your friendship with us in this school. As I have told you, with us as your companions, you have nothing to fear in this school. Your protection is fully assured. Just make sure that you keep close association with us and not relent. We will make sure that you feel comfortable in this school." He said to the others:

"Boys, isn't it so?"

"You are right," they echoed.

"All you have to do to continue to be our friend is to abide by our rules and regulations and always do our biddings, which we know will not be difficult for you. From today, you are our full-fledged friend, companion and members."

Ikenna asked the group what nickname that they thought Chibuogwum should bear. They each came up with many suggestions. At last, they settled upon the nickname "Little Tiger." From that very day onwards, they started referring to him or addressing him as "Little Tiger."

They continued to drink and to smoke, enjoying themselves, so they thought.

"Feel free and comfortable," Ikenna said to Chibuogwum as he sat beside him, the two holding cups of drink in their hands. "All these persons here are now your friends. You've been formally inducted into our group, and I assure you that you will certainly enjoy our company to the full. All of us are very nice persons." He smoked his cigarette as he talked to Chibuogwum. Chibuogwum sat quietly and listened attentively to all that Ikenna said.

It was evening. Chibuogwum and Ikenna lied down on the latter's bed, talking.

"I hope that you truly enjoyed the gathering we had just yesterday?"

"Yes, it was really lovely, exciting and so enjoyable," Chibuogwum replied excitedly and smiled joyfully. "I really like it and wish to have more of it."

"I told you so. I told you that you would enjoy our friendship, and you are already beginning to see the truthfulness of what I told you. In fact, you've not seen anything. You will still get more enjoyment if you remain with us. We are wonderful fellows. We will make your life worth while. You are going to experience true independence as you associate with us. We will add real meaning to your life. As you see, we have all it takes to be happy and unworried in this school."

"I just discovered so that day," Chibuogwum said.

Ikenna continue to talk excitedly to Chibuogwum about how good their group was. Chibuogwum listened with rapt attention, almost spell bound. He totally absorbed all Ikenna said as true and completely fascinated. His attention was wholly captured by the glowing things that Ikenna said of their group. Ikenna went on enumerating to Chibuogwum, benefits to be derived from the group. Chibuogwum was much pleased by what he heard and felt grateful to have been adopted into the group.

"I have something with which to spend our time together here," Ikenna announced. He got up from the bed and made towards his cupboard. He brought out a bottle of hot alcoholic drink and two small glass cups from it and deposited them on the small wooden stool on which Chibuogwum had sat during his previous visit. The two young men sat on the bed. Ikenna uncorked the crown of the bottle and added into it a substance known only by him. Then, he cocked the bottle's crown again and shook it vigorously. It foamed slightly. Next, he filled the two small glass cups with it. He took one of the cups and told Chibuogwum to have the other. Chibuogwum complied, they each began to sip the drink.

"You see, this life is full of enjoyment. You can make life whatever you want it to be," Ikenna said as they drank. "You do not need anyone to tell you how to live your life. It is your life, and it is your right to live it anyhow you like. To enjoy your life, you must allow no one to impose any unnecessary laws and restrictions on you, if they will obstruct your freedom and enjoyment. You don't need to be entangled by any rules. Do you understand?"

Chibuogwum nodded agreeably, "I believe your words are truth. I'm beginning to experience that so far."

"It is because I love you that I decided to introduce you to our way of life. Not only that you will enjoy life if you keep company with us, you will also be bold and courageous. With those attributes, nobody can intimidate you or make life unbearable for you."

"I believe that you are right, senior. I am glad to have you as my friend in this school. Chika has already told me many good things about you."

"Is Chika your friend?"

"Yes, he is my friend. He is the first person that approached me for friendship and told me many things about this school and the challenges that the junior students in this school face and also proferred solution to them. He always speaks highly and so nicely of you."

"Yes, Chika is my boy, just like you are now," Ikenna said. "And he is a nice boy as well. He is both obedient, intelligent and smart. If you adopt his way in your friendship with me and my friends, who are now also your friends, it will be well with you. It is good that you have said it with your own mouth that somebody, your friend, confirmed to you that I am a nice fellow, and good to be with."

"Indeed, I have observed that," Chibuogwum declared. "And as I've told you, I am so happy and grateful that we are friends, especially as I am now sure that nobody will maltreatment me in this school anymore."

"My boy, I love all that you've said. Remember that I am the great python. I swallow anything that stands in my way. Therefore, you have nothing to be frightened of. Well, you are now a little tiger, and that should give you the audacity you need to face any encounter."

They kept sipping their drinks from time to time. Ikenna's cup reduced and he refilled it up. Chibuogwum's own also had almost gone half. Senior Ikenna asked him if he needed more. Chibuogwum shook his head by way of answering in the negativity. From his looks, it was obvious that Chibuogwum was gradually getting intoxicated. His eyes were gradually turning a little reddish, and blurred. And he started to feel that his head was spinning and that it had been detached from his body. He also began to feel numbness in his feet and hands. He initially wanted to complain to senior Ikenna, but on a second thought, decided to keep quiet and pretend to be okay. He did not want Ikenna to think that he was unfit to be his friend. He wanted to please Ikenna by all possible means, no matter what could be the ramifications.

Ikenna on his part, although had begun to notice that the drinks was already beginning to have a toll on Chibuogwum, decided to pretend not to have observed anything. He kept talking pleasantly and excitedly to Chibuogwum.

At last, when Chibuogwum could no longer endure how he was feelings in silence, he spoke.

"Senior, I don't know how I am feeling," he said.

"What's the problem? How are you feeling?" Ikenna feigned surprised.

"I think I'm getting intoxicated," Chibuogwum stated.

"But you have just consumed a very lite quantity. Maybe you have little brains. You can lie down on the bed and see if you can sleep. That may help," Ikenna suggested.

Chibuogwum then lied down, and shortly afterwards, dozed off. Chibuogwum's association with the group was beginning to have pernicious influence on him.

CHAPTER EIGHT

I t was around nine O'clock in the night. The sky was clear and the mood was bright and shone brilliantly, illuminating everywhere. The breeze of that very night blew gently, soothing and caressing the body so lovely. Okereke, his wife and their little girl all sat outside on a big local mat, which was spread on the ground, to get the fresh and natural air of the night. They had just had their supper of pounded maize and vegetable sauce, prepare with maize and vegetables that Okereke and Uloaku his wife harvested from their garden. The girl was their last child. She was born a few years after the triplet – Chibuogwum, Chimankpam and Chinagorom – were born. Unlike her elder brothers and sister, she was still attending primary school from home. Her elder ones were in JSS One, all newly admitted. It was only Chibuogwum that was in a boarding school. The others attended school from home.

The little girl whose name was Udodirim had in the day time requested her father to tell her folktales. Okereke her father had promised her that he would do that in the night. So, they were outside that night to fulfill his promise to tell the little Udodirim folktales. In fact, Okereke was a treasury of folktales. He had learned most of the folk stories that he usually told from his own father, who was himself a renowned story teller too. Not only that, he also inherited from him his masterful and superb art of story telling. All that he needed to display his unique art of story telling, with which he was endowed, was only a simple request to tell stories. He could tell hundreds of good, didactic and entertaining stories that people, mainly little children, took delight in listening to.

"Once upon a time, long, very long ago," he began. "Long ago when animals talked as humans and when if one was feeling hungry, could cut out part of the heaven and eat. There was a famine in the land of the animals."

"I hope it is not the one about the Tortoise and the elephant and the spirit being? Or the one about the he-goat and the spirits' cloth? I don't want them again. I have heard them so many times," Udodirim protested. "Tell me a new story," she added, as if warning her father.

Okereke chuckled. "Ok, my daughter. I will tell you a new and enthralling folktale tonight. It will make you really glad. You have not heard the one that I am going to tell you tonight before. It is one of my best stories, and I rarely tell it to people," Okereke assured Udodirim.

"That's good, father," Udodirim admitted blissfully.

"Once upon a time, a very long time ago, in the land of the animals, there occurred a severe famine," he began again. "All the animals, including the Tortoise, suffered greatly as a result. Tortoise looked weak and grew thin in his shell for lack of food. All the animals, including the birds, suffered severally. Some of them even died.

One day, seeing the suffering of the birds as a result of the famine, the people of the heaven specially invited the birds to a feast in the sky. The birds were much excited at the prospect of going to heaven and enjoying sumptuous meals and began to get prepared for the appointed day. The birds all gathered at their village square and discussed how they would attend the feast in the sky.

Soon, the Tortoise saw all that was going on and enquired what it was all about. He was told what was happening. From the moment he got the information, he started longing to attend the feast in the sky with the birds. Although Tortoise was not a bird but a land animal, nonetheless, he decided to go to the birds and ask them for permission to join them in attending the feast in the sky. He had already begun to imagine the type of food and drinks that they might be served with. He told the birds that he wanted to attend the feast in the heaven with them.

After listening carefully to him, the leader of the birds said to him:

'We know the kind of person you are very well. You are a cheat and unthankful creature. If we permit you to go with us, you surely will be up to deceit. You are wicked and ungrateful. So, we will not allow you to go with us.'

"The Tortoise tried to convince the birds that he was a changed person."

'You are not correct, my friends,' Tortoise replied to the birds.' I have changed; I am no longer what I used to be. I have learned that anyone who is doing evil to others or cheating others is doing so to himself and that whatever you wish others is what will come upon you. I'm now a good and trustworthy persons that shun evil.'

"The Tortoise's tongue was sweet. After hearing his speech, the birds believed that he had actually changed his bad ways and manners. They all agreed to let him go with them. But how would he be able to fly to the sky since Tortoise was not a bird but a land animal? Each of the birds gave him a feather, and with the feathers, he made two wings. The Tortoise stood out amongst the other birds, handsome in his multi – coloured plumage.

"When the appointed day came, the birds set off for the sky, with the Tortoise in their midst. He was so happy to be with the birds, to be flying like the birds and to be attending the feast. He was full of joy and was talkative.

'When people are invited to feasts as this, their hosts expect them to take new names,' Tortoise said to the birds. 'Our hosts too will expect us to honour this custom.'

"None of the birds had heard of this custom. But since Tortoise was a wise animal and widely travelled, they thought he must know the customs of many people. So, in obedience to this custom, the birds each took a new name for the occasion. Tortoise chose to be called "All of You." Tortoise talked excitedly as he flew with the birds and told them many delightful stories that relished them. The birds listened to his stories with rapt attention and undivided interested.

At last, the party arrived at the sky where they were invited for a feast. Because of his unique appearance, the people of the heaven thought that the Tortoise was the leader or king of the birds. Therefore, they appointed him over the birds.

Tortoise was an experienced and a great orator that spoke with grace and ease, letting his words flow freely to the utmost admiration of his audience. The birds and the people of the heaven listened to him spell bound. He thanked the people of the heaven for organizing the feast for them and promised that they would do their best to keep the relationship between the birds and the people of the heaven strong.

Due to his eloquence, the birds felt very proud to have brought him and immensely applauded him. The people of the heaven too were amazed at his speech that they also applauded him.

When time for the hosts to serve their guests with food and drinks came, they set before the birds the most delicious food and rich wine Tortoise had ever seen. There were foofoo, garri, pounded yam with egusi soup; (melon) and bitter leaves and ogbono soup; yam porridge, rice and stew, beans, bean pudding, real palm wine – straight from the raffia palm tree, meat and fish. There were also assorted drinks and kolanuts, fruits and other delicious meals.

Tortoise began to salivate upon seeing those things. He was now full of greed once more. Turning to their hosts, he asked:

'Whom have you prepared all these for?' Tortoise asked, pointing at the food and drinks.

'For all of you," the people of the heaven answered.

"Father, this one is interesting," Udodirim remarked joyfully. "It is different from the ones you've told me before."

"That's nice," Okereke noted, almost in whispers. He went on with the folktale.

"Turning to the birds, Tortoise said:

'You remember that my name is All of You. Also, here, it is the custom to serve the spokesperson and the leader first. As you've heard from our hosts, all these food and drinks and other things belong to All of You, which is my name – me.'

"With that, Tortoise settled down at the table and began to enjoy himself with the food and drinks and other things provided for them by theirs hosts. The birds watched him in anger as he ate and drank, feeling hungry and salivating too. They started to regret having brought him along. On the other hand, the people of the heaven didn't intervene, for they thought it was the custom of the birds to let their king eat first. Tortoise ate and ate and ate and drank and drank and drank until his belly was full of foods and drinks and his body swelled up to his shell.

"When he had had his fil, he left what remained for the birds, including bones. They were too annoyed to taste anything. However, some of them that could not stand hunger striking them pecked at the bones and ate the food he left and drank the wine he left behind. Those that refused to eat the food that Tortoise left, decided to return hungry. They were all annoyed at Tortoise's behaviour, but Parrot was mostly annoyed."

"The birds all agreed to punish Tortoise. They each collected back from him the feathers they'd given him. He stood in his shell with his body full of food and drinks, but with no wings to fly back home. When he saw what the birds had done to him, he did not know what to do. He begged the birds to deliver a message to his wife, but they all refused. However, at last, the parrot who had felt much angrier than the other birds, suddenly had a change of mind and accepted to take Tortoise's message to his wife.

'Tell my wife to bring out all the soft things in the house and spread in the compound, so that when I jump down from here, I will not get hurt; Tortoise said to parrot.

"Parrot agreed to deliver Tortoise's message to Tortoise's wife. But when Parrot got to Tortoise's house, he told Tortoise's wife that her husband asked her to bring out all the hard things in the house and spread them in the compound.

"The Tortoise's wife in obedience to what was said to be her husband's message, brought out all the hard things in their house, including hoes, matches, spears and spread them in the compound.

"The Tortoise looked down from the sky and saw his wife bringing things out. But because it was very far he could not see clearly what they were. He thought Parrot delivered his message to his wife exactly as he had given it, not knowing that his wife was being given a different and wrong message altogether. He watched his wife from the heaven. When everything seemed to have been ready, he made a jump from the sky.

"He began to tall and to fall and to fall and to fall, until it seemed to him that getting to the ground was impossible, as the sky was so far from the ground. He thought he was finished. At last, he landed on the ground in his compound. It sounded like the blast of atomic bomb. His shell broke into pieces, but he survived.

"Then, he consulted snail, the priest doctor, and he patched up his shell for him. That is why Tortoise had rough shell," Okereke concluded his folktale.

"This very one is nice," Udodirim said amid laughter. "I like it."

"Didn't I tell you that the story I was about to narrate to you would be of great interest to you?" Okereke asked rhetorically.

"You did. Tell me another interesting tale," Udodirim requested.

"Okay, I will tell you another story," Mazi Okereke accepted. "After, you tell me the lessons you learned."

"I will do that, father," Udodirim said.

"Once upon a time," he began. "There was a famine in the land of the animals."

"Father, your tales are all almost about famine in the land of the animals. Why?" Udodirim observed.

"Because it is their common problem," Mazi Okereke replied.

"I see," Udodirim gave up.

"The Tortoise had nothing to eat. So, one day, he went into the bush in search of what to eat. He went from palm tree to palm tree to see if he could pick up some palm fruits to eat.

"The first palm tree he came to had nothing and he cursed it. He went on to the next. It had palm heads, but they had not ripened. His luck turned when he arrived at the third palm tree. He saw plenty of ripe nuts on the ground. He looked up and also saw two or three ripe palm heads on the tree. He picked up some of the fallen palm fruits and ate them. He wanted to have all the palm fruits for himself. Therefore, he climbed the palm tree, cut down one of the palm heads, and it fell to the ground.

The Tortoise came down from the palm tree. Something strange occurred. He could not find the palm head he had cut. He searched for it everywhere, but could not find it. Tortoise was bewildered. He saw a big hole nearby and thought that the palm head might have fallen into it. He decided to go into it in search of his palm head. As he went down, the hole led deep down into the bottom of the earth. Tortoise went on, determined to find his missing palm head.

Not long, he came in contact with some spirit – looking beings. They we're gathered round his palm head, eating it.

"Tortoise was surprised. 'What are you doing?' Tortoise exclaimed. "The plan head is mine. Give back to me.'

"As the spirit saw Tortoise, they ran away. They went to their King and reported. The King ordered that the Tortoise be brought before his presence.

"When Tortoise appeared before the King, he said, bowing."
'Your Majesty, you will live forever.'
'What brought you here?' the King enquired.
'I want the palm head and the nuts back because it was hunger that drove me put of my house to cut it,' the Tortoise replied.

'Since you've identified hunger as your major problem, I have a solution to it," the King said. He ordered his servants to give Tortoise a magic drum. Tortoise was instructed to tap the drum any time he felt hungry, that food would come out. Tortoise thanked the King and departed with the magic drum.

"On getting out of the hole, Tortoise tapped the drum. Something wonderful occurred. Different types of food, drinks and fruits came out of it. Tortoise could not believed his eyes. He tasted the food, drinks and fruits. It was real food, deliciously prepared, so tasty. Tortoise nodded satisfactorily. He ate as much as he could and then took the drum home. It was incredible.

"On arriving home, he summoned his wife and other members of his family and told them to wash the plates, pots, cups and spoons because food was coming. Initially, they doubted him, but remembering that Tortoise was both a well travelled and a wise man, they obeyed him.

"Tortoise hit the drum. Something astonishing took place before all. Food was everywhere. Everyone ate as much as he or she wanted.

"The next day, Tortoise invited all the animals to have a share of his good fortune. He told the animals that he had found remedy to the severe famine that had ravaged their lives. The animals gathered and looked on to see what Tortoise would do.

"Tortoise gently hit the drum. What the animals saw amazed them. Food of every type appeared, enough to satisfy all the animals, and surplus. The animals descended on the food and drinks hungrily and had their very fills. They all thanked Tortoise.

"However, elephant did not attend the gathering, for he was not informed on time. But on getting to hear what had happened, he resolved that he would not be left out. He wanted his own share of the food and drinks. So, he went down to Tortoise's house. But when he arrived, Tortoise was not at home. He met only Tortoise's wife. The elephant persuaded Tortoise's wife to give him the drum. At last, she succumbed and gave him the magic drum. The elephant hit it hard. Food came out. He ate and ate. He kept hitting the drum and at last hit it very hard. The drum broke. Food stopped flowing out.

"When Tortoise returned home, he saw that everywhere was quiet. He enquired what had happened, and he was told that the elephant had broken the magic drum.

"Upon hearing that, Tortoise became infuriated at the elephant. However, on a second thought which was that he could still get another one, his annoyance abated.

"He returned to the same palm tree. This time, it had no ripe heads on it. Nonetheless, Tortoise climbed it and cut down a palm head. He did not even care to know whether it was ripe or not. He came down, and saw the palm head exactly where it had fallen. Tortoise threw it into the hole. He went down into hole. He went straight to the King and complained that his subjects had taken his palm head. The King issued an order that Tortoise's palm head be given back to him. But Tortoise objected.

'I want another drum, instead,' Tortoise requested. Without the least hesitation, the King agreed and gave him another drum. However, he told him not to tap the drum until he had gone out of the kingdom. Tortoise was full of joy to have got another drum, which meant more food and drinks

"As soon as he left the spirits' realm, he tapped the drum. Bees and wasps – angry, buzzing ones, filled everywhere. They stung Tortoise on all his body. He withdrew into his shell. But some of them managed to enter there. Tortoise started to roll on the ground in pains. Suddenly, he stumbled upon the drum. The bees and wasps disappeared. His body was swollen as a result of the bees' stings. Tortoise could hardly walk. He only managed to crawl back home with the drum.

"Tortoise arrived home later. He did not let his family members experience what he had experienced. Straight away, he assembled the animals. The attendance was immense. Everyone turned up, ready to share in the free food. Tortoise brought out the drum. He only gave them one instruction to observe. They should not hit the drum until he had climbed half of the tree at the back of his compound. He had already told the members of his family to vacate the compound. They obeyed and sneaked out of the compound through the back door of his house.

"All the animals watched as Tortoise slowly climbed the tree. The elephant, the lion, the tiger, the gorilla, monkey, dogs, pigs, and other animals were all there. Nobody wanted to be left out.

"When the animals saw that Tortoise had climbed half way up the tree, they could wait no more. They hit the drum mightily. Bees and wasps appeared in large number and descended on the animals, stinging hard on them. The elephant, being the most huge of all the animals, suffered more than the other animals from the wasps' and bees' stings. In his effort to get away, the elephant trampled many little animals underfoot. All the animals tried to get away, the lion, the tiger, the gorilla, the monkey, the dogs, pigs, and a host of others. There was a great stampede as the animals tried to escape to safety. The bees and wasps stung them all over their bodies, so painful.

"From the top of the tree, Tortoise watched the animals with great amusement. He laughed at them derisively. In fact, what happened to the animals that day was extremely indescribable.

They regretted having come to answer Tortoise's call and had no mouth with which to narrate what they passed through.

"At last, one of the animals stumbled on the drum mistakenly. The bees and wasps disappeared instantly. Then, the animals got relieved. Those that survived hurried back to their various abodes in tears.

"That's the end of the folk story," Okereke announced finally. "What lessons did you learn from the two stories I have related to you tonight?"

"I learn that it is bad to pay back good with evil as the Tortoise did to the birds. I also learned that it is good to be industrious and hardworking. It is also not good to make others suffer misfortunes with us. I also learned that it is better to work to get our own food rather than depending on getting things free. Further, we should avoid cheating others. Those are what I have learned from the folktales you've told," Udodirim concluded.

"That's very good of you, my beloved daughter," Okereke extoled. "You have truly derived invaluable lessons from the stories. That indicates that you listened very well to the stories as they were being told. You are truly an intelligent child."

It was about half – pass ten. Uloaku was already feeling sleepy. She too had listened to the stories with interest and had liked them.

"We have to go in now," Uloaku reminded Okereke. "It is late into the night already. Udodirim will still go to school tomorrow. So, let her go and sleep. You can to tell her more stories another day."

"You are right. Let's go in," Mazi Okekere accepted. "I did not even know that it is already passed ten O'clock."

They all got up and walked in, Uloaku still feeling sleepy, rubbing her eyes with the back of her hands.

The stories that Okereke told had exquisitely thrilled and delighted Udodirim, that she kept pondering them to the extent that she had a series of dreams about it throughout that very night.

CHAPTER NINE

In the school, Chibuogwum's friendship with Ikenna and other members of the group had grown very strong. The gangsters gathered together on regular basis. Chibuogwum, Chika and Ikenna, especially had developed a special and unique bond. Wherever one of them was seen, the others must be there. Their friendship was seen and noted by all in the school, including the teachers. But none, except those that belonged to their group knew what went on in secret. Chibuogwum was now wholly enticed by the spurious enjoyment of the group.

Chika, Chibuogwum's friend, was an only son. Like Chibuogwum, his parents were childless for years before being blessed with him. As an only child, his parents were determined to give him the best in life that they could afford, especially good education. So, they had admitted him to this prestigious boarding school for high quality education with which he could face any test in future and be truly successful. His parents wanted the best for him. Of course, all the parents that sent their children to the school wanted the best for them. That was why they did not mind paying huge sums of money each term for their education without feeling overwhelmed or begrudge doing so. They did that with sincere cheers, hopeful that they were laying fine foundation for their children future.

Unlike Chibuogwum that got admitted into the school completely by merit because he was intelligent, Chika's father had had to offer something for kola to the principal to see Chika through in the admission. He had come short of the required grade for admission into the school with a few marks during the school's entrance examination. His father very much wanted him to be in that school, at least to feel the pride or happiness that was often seemed to be attached to those whose children were there. He wanted nothing less than the best for his son, mainly since he had waited for years before God blessed him with him.

Prior to Chika's birth, his parents had been childless and had visited many places for help or solution, including priest or juju doctors. The priest doctor that they had consulted was Okaka.

After consulting his oracles, he told them what the spirits said. He attributed their childless state to his late father, whose proper funeral rites he had not duly performed. Chika's father had asked the priest doctor what could be done. The priest doctor had replied that the spirit of his late father needed to be appeased with a sacrifice. Chika's father had asked him what were required for the sacrifice.

The priest doctor had then prescribed to him the requirement for the sacrifice. He provided the items that the priest doctor had requested by paying for them without even the least reluctance. He was more than willing to offer anything, even all he and in exchange for a child of his own. Few days later, the sacrifice had been carried out. The priest doctor had assured Chika's father that in a year, his wife would conceive. However, more than one year passed, but nothing happened.

But all hope was not lost. They visited the second herbalist. This very one had combined traditional medicine of roots and leaves with spiritual powers. He had told him that his wife had a spiritual husband without knowing, and that she had been bearing him children without knowing too. He had said that a sacrifice needed to be offered to enable him wage a powerful battle with the strong powers of the spiritual husband. After, he would give them medicine of roots and leaves. He had claimed to have possessed the power to fight this spiritual husband and conquer him. Without hesitation, Chika's parents had provided everything that the priest doctor had asked for. The sacrifice was done, but still nothing happened.

Still, they did not give up. They consulted the third priest doctor. After doing the incantation and talking with the spirits, he had attributed their childlessness to wicked machinations or works of those that hated them. He went on and assured them that he would use his strong spiritual powers to render their powers powerless and bring joy into their relationship. He had told them what he needed for a sacrifice to destroy the works of their enemies, and they had given them without objection.

The priest doctor had taken Chika's mother to a river located very far from where people in the village lived at midnight and had her bathed with the blood of a bull that they had slaughtered for the sacrifice, in the presence of her husband and the priest doctor, fully naked under light from candles of different colours and the bright moonlight. The priest doctor had even gone as far as helping her to bathe, occasionally touching her intimate parts. The husband did not mind. All that he needed was a child of their own. He didn't care, if that could give them what they wanted.

In spite of all that, it ended just as others – fruitless. Although they were successful materially, they had no real joy as their childlessness had rendered their conjugal life imperfect, incomplete and almost void. After all the priest doctors he visited had done their works with no result, they decided to try orthodox medicine.

There was one popular doctor in town about this time. He was a well – known gynaecologist and obstetrician. Because of his professionalism in his field of specialization, he was popularly called Dr. Special. But his real name was Dr. Chibueze. He was a stoutly built young man of average height in his mid-forties, with four children. His name as a doctor had quickly spread very far like wild fire at harmattan season. People trooped to his clinic like soldier ants in search of remedy to their gynaecological and obstetric problems, especially women.

It was this doctor that Chika's parents had decided to turn to for help. Patience was to visit him alone as George was extremely busy with his business the day they had scheduled to consult him. On that very day, she arrived at the clinic at around 07:40 a.m. She had woken up early and got breakfast ready for her husband and herself. She was not used to taking breakfast at early morning, but on the that very day, she'd decided to break that custom in case some medicinal drugs were needed to be administered to her. She had simply taken a breakfast of a cup of tea and some slices of bread, garnished with fried eggs and butter. She wanted to get to the hospital on time in order to be among the first set of patients to see the doctor as the doctor had to attend to countless patients each day. Although consultation with the doctor usually started at 08:00 a.m. and that she had arrived as early as 07:40 a.m, the clinic was already almost filled with patients waiting to see the doctor.

In order to reduce quarreling and unnecessary bickerings among patients as to who would see the doctor first, the clinic had adopted the strategy of giving numbers to the patients. Although she had arrived on time, Patience only managed to be number 38. She did not know that giving numbers to the patients started as early as 07:00 a.m. When her turn came, she paid her fee for card to the clinic clerk, who issued her with a receipt and card with a number.

Being the 38th person to see the doctor, she knew quite well that she had to wait for hours before she could see the doctor. Therefore, she went to the waiting hall and sat down with other patients who were also waiting to see the doctor. In order to facilitate the time, she had brought out her Android phone and began watching films that she had downloaded already. Even though the clinic bustled with patients and staff of the clinic, she was oblivious of all that as she was busy operating her phone, her mind being completely arrested.

Finally, her turn to see the doctor came. She went to the door of the doctor's consultation room and tapped on it gently. A low but deep male voice, said from within:

"Come in,"

Patience opened the door gently and her face came in direct contact with the doctor's as she entered. She greeted the doctor who replied and waved her to a seat opposite him and sat back in his easy-chair. He fixed her with a gaze. He was sitting behind a large table.

"Young woman, what is your problem?" He asked.

"I have been married for years without a child," Patience had replied after sitting down.

The doctor looked at her sympathetically and with admiration for her striking beauty. He had noticed that she was tall, well-built and beautiful created. In his heart, he praised God for such a pretty work. He wondered why most of those that came to him for child problem were pretty women. He wondered if it was God's will that nobody could have everything in this life in totality. Here was a young woman, so beautiful and materially buoyant, yet she lacked a child, and was sad for it. Of course, he was used to meeting that kind of condition.

"How long have you been married without conceiving?" He asked in a gentle voice as he still fixed Patience with a gaze as if he was expecting to get the answer to his question from her body.

"Fourteen years, doctor," Patience replied. She mopped her face with a handkerchief as sweat had started gathering on her face. The doctor allowed her to finish before coming with yet another question.

"Have you ever been pregnant, even before you got married?" the doctor asked further.

Patience was hesitant. She began to think what could have prompted the doctor to ask such question. She felt that he had put the question to her to find out if she had damaged her womb during abortion of unwonted pregnancy or something similar. After pondering that in her mind, she said:

"No, doctor,"

"Have you ever had such ailments as kidney problem, tuberculosis or undergone any surgical operations in the past?

"No, doctor."

"Have you ever consulted a doctor to know if your womb is ok?"

"No, doctor. You are the first medical doctor that I've ever visited with this problem of mine," Patience slowly explained in reply, almost taking the words one after the other.

The doctor sat forward, bent towards the table in front of him and began to write on the patient's file. After writing, he went on with his inquisition.

"What about your husband? Has he ever consulted a medical professional to ascertain the status of his manhood?"

"Yes, doctor. About eight years ago, and the doctor confirmed him all right?"

"Okay," said the doctor as he kept writing down things. "Nevertheless, both of you need to be examined again to make sure that all is normal with you. You will have to come back next week. Bring your husband along. Two of you will be medically examined. "I hope he will agree to come with you? Or if you like, I can conduct your own examination now, then next week when you'll come with your husband, he will do his own."

She thought. "Let's do the examination together next week," Patience replied. "Surely, he will come with me. He was the one that suggested my coming here to see you. He will never object if it will bring the desired result."

"You've to make some deposit so that when you return next week, everything will move smoothly."

"How much should I deposit, doctor," Patience asked.

"Forty Thousand Naira, if you can afford that now," the doctor answered.

"Do you accept bank transfer?" Patience asked.

"Yes, we do accept bank transfer," Dr. Special said in response "Go to the clerk and get our account details from him."

They came to the hospital as scheduled and had the examinations conducted on them. The results came out, and they were both reported normal. Notwithstanding, the doctor prescribed some drugs for them and referred them to the dispensary for collection of the drugs he had prescribed for them. They collected the drugs, went home and used them as directed. Yet, nothing positive took place. They consulted a few more medical practioners and then decided to give up making further efforts to solve their problem. They concluded that the best thing to do was to commit everything about their plight into God's hands and wait for his time.

It was at the time when all hope seemed to have been lost that an unexpected miracle took place. One early morning, Patience had something to tell her husband, George.

"I missed my menstruation this month," she had complained as they were lying on the bed. "I was supposed to have it last week." She explained.

"You missed your period?" George repeated by way of reply. "What do you think that indicates?"

"I don't know," Patience replied.

"May be we will consult a doctor to know what the cause is," she suggested.

"Ok," George agreed.

Later on, a doctor was consulted, and she was found to be pregnant. The couple rejoiced greatly and thanked God. George particular thanked God for making his wife to become pregnant after many years of fruitless search for a child of their own. Nine months after, Patience was delivered of a baby boy and they named him Chika. They invited friends and well wisher to a lavish party to celebrate, thank God and rejoice with them.

They were grateful to God for blessing them with a child of their own.

CHAPTER TEN

Chibuogwum's group in the school scheduled a meeting in which they would plan on how to carry out their operation. They had invited Chibuogwum to attend. It was Ikenna that personally gave him the invitation. This was Chibuogwum's first time joining them in their operations. The group gathered at the usual uncompleted building to plan how to carry out their nefarious activities. Senior Ikenna stood in front of them as they assembled, addressing them. It was around 12:30 a.m.

"Great dragons!" Ikenna saluted

"Oneness!" The group replied

"Great dragons!"

"Unity of actions!"

"Great dragons!"

"Be your brother's keeper!"

"I happily welcome you all to this all important meeting. The aim of this meeting is to plan on how to keep this club moving. As you might have observed, we've not engaged in any operation by which we maintain this group financially, and I feel that it is time to call a meeting for that purpose. You might have noticed too that we have someone in our midst who is totally new to this group and a novice too. But I can attest that he is bold, courageous and determined to adapt to the life style of this group. He has indeed proven to me that he can relate well with us if properly trained and guided aright. It was at our last gathering that I introduced him to this group, and we all officially welcomed him. I've tested and interviewed him and also trained him, and I found him fit. As you all know not all of us will participate in the operation. Only five persons will go." He selected five persons for the operation. Chibuogwum was among them.

"I will lead them in the operation, while the rest of us will remain here. You may recall that those that I did not select have all participated in their own operations in the past." He paused. "But before we leave, I will like us to enjoy ourselves a little. To that end, I have brought some drinks with me to this place. "He brought out two bottles of hot drink of different brands from a bag in front of him and placed them at the centre. He ordered Chibugowm to share the drink to all of them.

They all started to drink and to dance, to their very pleasure. After a few minutes of enjoying themselves, they got ready and left for the operation zone, stealthily and determined. They returned safely before dawn, heavily moneyed. They assembled the following night and celebrated their success extravagantly. They drank and smoked uncontrollably in secret. In all this, none in the school, not even the principal and the teachers, knew about Ikenna's group and its activities, except the members.

But one day, something that altered and devastated Chibuogwum's whole life happened. The principal invited him to his office and informed him that he had got a letter from his mother asking him to come home the next day. Chibuogwum was surprised at such sudden and urgent message, requiring him to come home quickly. His mind went to many things that could have promoted that type of message. His mind wandered very wild the night before the day of his departure, that he had a series of dreams, some of them frightening.

The following day, he got prepared and went home. On his arrival, he met his mother and many others in the compound, all in unhappy moods. All of them were sorrowing. Upon enquiry, he learned that his father had died in an auto crash on a business trip two days earlier and was deposited in a mortuary to await proper funeral rites. Everyone mourned and wept. The compound was filled with sympathizers and comforters. Chibuogwum cried and cried and cried until his eyes turned sore. His mother also wept uncontrollably and people tried very hard to comfort her. Everyone was amazed at Okereke's sudden death and rendered speechless. Chibuogwum's younger ones also cried heavily over their father's painful death.

Three weeks later, the burial took place. He was committed to mother earth amidst wailings from family members, relations and lovers. People wept uncontrollably. Some even dashed themselves on the ground. Uloaku wept her eyes to soreness and tried to throw herself into the grave but was restrained. The funeral rites were later performed.

Okereke's demise marked the end of Chibuogwum's schooling at the boarding school. After some time, he went back to the boarding school in the company of his mother, Uloaku and they collected his belongings back home. The principal, the teachers and his fellow students that saw them immensely consoled them, especially Chibuogwum, over the passing away of his father. Few days after his return, Chibuogwum was enrolled in a day school that he would be attending from home like his sisters.

It was around 2p.m. Chibuogwum could see smoke coming out from their kitchen's roof, as he was returning from school. Chibuogwum was now in JSS two. He knew why the smoke was coming out of their kitchen – his mother was preparing lunch for him and for other members of the family. He had never been starved before, for Uloaku his mother, always made sure that his food was ready before he returned from school.

As he approached the house, he turned towards the kitchen, where he found his mother dishing out lunch of pounded maize, wrapped in banana leaves and sauce prepared with pumpkin vegetables, into plates for the family consumption. He greeted her and went into the main house to change his school uniform. Before he came into the kitchen, he could perceive the sweet aroma of the sauce that was to be used in eating the pounded maize, and was happy as a result

Chibuogwum, after about five minutes, came back into the kitchen to collect his own portion of the food. Uloaku who was sitting on a small chair, gave a ball of pounded maize wrapped in banana leaves, tied with tender palm leaves and boiled like that which she put into a plate to Chibuogwum. She also took another plate and ladled the sauce into it and also gave it to Chibuogwum, who accepted it appreciatively.

"Thanks Ma," Chibuogwum greeted his mother as he took the plates of food and sat down on a chair beside his mother to begin eating. Chibuogwum ate with gusto, licking his fingers noisily to show that the food was very tasty. In a few minutes, it remained a little for the food to finish. Uloaku's mind told her that the food she had given to her son might not be sufficient to feed him well. So, she asked Chibuogwum:

"Chibuogwum, do you need more?"

"No, this is enough," Chibuogwum replied. "I'm already well-fed."

"You know that I love you so much because you are my only son. You are my only hope and my husband too. You know your father is no more. You are the only thing so valuable I have now, and I will make sure I give you all you want. If only your father was alive..."

"Oh, no, mother," Chibuogwum interrupted her. "Stop talking like that. You don't need to get worried because father is dead."

"Your father was a nice person; he cared for us very well," Uloaku said as tears rolled down her cheeks. "Oh, death, see what you have done to me, a poor young woman. You have made me a widow, when my age mates are enjoying their marriages with their husbands. You are so callous."

"Stop doing this, mother," Chibuogwum said, "I will make it up for you. God will use me to bring comfort to you. In fact, mother I promise to take good care of you when I grow up. I will buy luxurious cars for you and get you a competent driver to drive you around and to anywhere you want to go. I will get house helps for you, build large – beautiful houses for you, buy jet, aeroplane and helicopter for you so that if there is traffic jam, you can use any of them to get to where you are going fastly. In short, when I grow up, your suffering will cease."

"My good son," Uloaku said. "You have brought hope and joy into my life with these your promises. God will guide and help you to fulfill them. You have just shown me that you love me so much and that you will be a useful person in life when you grow, with these promises you have made. God will surely see to it that you do what you have promised me. That's my sincere prayer."

"Amen," Chibuogwum answered in affirmation of what Uloaku uttered.

"God is aware of my situation, and he will comfort me through you, as you have said," Uloaku said. "God will not let me continue to suffer forever."

"Yes, mother you are right. He will use me to renew your hope and wipe your tears. I will do many good things for you when I become adult."

"Oh, my son, come and hug me. You know your mother's heart. Good child."

Chibuogwum stood up and went to Uloaku and they embraced each other lovingly and warmly. At this juncture, Chibuogwum had already finished eating. After they had disengaged, Chibuogwum collected his plates together and was about to go inside and keep them so that he could wash them later. But Uloaku told him not to worry about that, that she would do that.

"But mother, I want to help you; it's my duty."

"Don't be bothered. I know that it is your responsibility. You have always washed plates in this house and I have never told you not to. Do you know why I did it now?"

"No mother. Why don't you want me to wash plates now?"

"It's because I'm glad for you because of the promises you made to me. It has truly gladdened my heart and illuminated my life."

"I'm happy to hear that, mother," Chibuogwum replied. "But I will be happier if you will allow me do it now to start helping you."

"Don't worry, my good son," Uloaku responded. "Let me do the washing now. Next time, you will have to wash them, ok?"

"Mother, I will not be happy if you do not permit me to do what I want to do."

"Alright, you can go ahead with the washing if you insist on so doing," Uloaku said resignedly.

Chibuogwum collected the plates together and went to the back of the kitchen to get them washed and rinsed. That his mother was glad because of the promises he made, lifted his spirit and made him felt loved and cherished. Of course, he was an only son, and was determined to wipe his mother's tears by fulfilling his promises when he grew up. He wished to make his mother happy, being the only son and the only hope of his mother in life.

Uloaku on her own side put her total trust in her son's childish promises, and thenceforth began to plan on how to reap the fruits of her labour through Chibuogwum. She was resolved to invest all her resources towards ensuring the success of her son and fulfillment of her son's excellent promises, which had begun to sweeten her sour life. The promises brought her genuine bliss and her view of Chibuogwum, her son, changed. She was so grateful to God that her relief from her plights and agonies in life would come through her only son. It had always been her prayer that her son would do good things for her and make her life luxuriant to compensate for her woes, miseries and distresses in her youthful age. Uloaku who often used to brood over her life's situation before her son's promises, drastically minimized its regularity.

7

When Chinagorom and Chimamkpam came into the kitchen and stood beside Uloaku on both sides, she did not notice their presence, for she was still contemplating on her life, especially over Chibuogwum's stupendous promises. They just stood quiet and watched their mother as she gesticulated for some minutes. Then, she looked at her both sides, and was amazed to see her daughters already standing beside her and realized that she had been deeply carried away in deep thought and engrossed in her private world.

8

"Oh, you are here? " she said to them in surprise. "Take your food and eat. I've been looking for you children. Where did you go to?"

"We were at Mama Adaku's house to play with our friend, Adaku," Chinagorom answered.

"Alright, take those plates of food and go and eat." She pointed at four plates of food a little distance in the front of her. Two plates contained the pounded maize and the remaining two contained sauce, with which to eat it. "Chinagorom, the ones at right are your own, and you, Chimamkpam, the ones at left belong to you. If you are not well-fed and satisfied after eating, you let me know so that I will give you more."

"Thanks, mother," Chinagorom and Chimamkpam greeted their mother simultaneously. They collected the plates of food and went to a place that would be comfortable and suitable for them to stay and enjoy the afternoon repast.

Uloaku watched them with absolute gladness and contentment, and believed they would enjoy the meal she had prepared.

She also started to develop hope in them to bring her fortunes in life, but not as strong as she put in Chibuogwum because of his gender. Chibuogwum was a boy and would be more useful than Chinagorom and Chimamkpam put together, for they are mere girls, and girls are inferior to boys, she thought within her.

CHAPTER ELEVEN

Chibuogwum had two friends called Ugonna and Uchenna. They were so close in their friendship,. They agreed virtually on everything and did everything together, and with one heart. They were almost the same age and came from the same village, and were also classmates.

One afternoon, during break at school, Uchenna and Ugonna went to an uncompleted building. They were there to stay alone and eat meat of big rat, which Uchenna's elder brother had killed. As Uchenna and Ugonna were eating the meat, Chibuogwum entered.

"Ugonna and Uchenna, I have been looking for you," Chibuogwum said to Uchenna and Ugonna. "And my mind told me that you must be here. Oh, you are eating meat. Who gave it to you?"

"It's my brother that killed it and cooked it and gave a portion to me. It is rat meat," Uchenna replied. "Take this and eat, it is very good." Uchenna gave a piece of meat to Chibuogwum.

"Uchenna," Ugonna called. "How does your elder brother kill all the big rats he kills?"

"Yes, that's a very good question you have asked, Ugonna," Chibuogwum supported. "Because I think we should learn how he does that and see if we can do it one day."

"It seems that you know what I have in mind for asking the question. It is important we know how he kills the rats, so that we can go and look for them and have them killed and get enough meat to eat, rather than relying on the little he gives to Uchenna, out of which he gives some pieces to us."

"You both are right," Uchenna said. "There was a day I accompanied my brother, Abuchi to a hunting expedition, and I watched him as he killed some big rats and also helped him. This is how he did the killing of rats the day I followed him in his hunting activities:

"My brother found a fairly big hole into which a big rat lived. He cleared its surroundings and used his machete to search for outlets from which the big rat may attempt to escape. After he had searched out the outlets, he cut some sticks and used them to block the holes. He then collected dried leaves and blocked the entrance hole with them. He also added some pepper to it and set fire to it, after which he blew off the flame and allowed only the smoke to appear and used a hand fan to fan the smoke into the hole. The animal inside the hole found it difficult to breathe and also felt uncomfortable and began to cough. And when it could no longer bear it, it sought to escape by speedily bursting out from the hole. Then, my brother caught it and bled it with his cutlass. That was what he did and killed some rats."

"I think with this information, we can kill a rat," Ugonna said.

"You are right," Chibuogwum said. "And it is not too difficult to do, based on how he has described how his brother killed his own rats. But where can we find holes in which rats live?"

"I have seen about three of them." Uchenna replied. "We can go now and kill the big rats inside them."

"How do you know that rats are living inside them? Do you think that it is in every hole that rats live?" Ugonna asked.

"I know how a hole into which a rat lives looks like," Uchenna replied. "The entrance looks smooth, with fresh kernels and palm fruits, the foot prints of the animal, some kinds of fruits and other things that show that something is living inside the hole. I found all these in each of the holes I am telling you about. So, we will succeed."

"Are you sure of what you are telling us?" Chibuogwum asked, "because I don't want to go there and toil myself for nothing."

"Yes I am sure," answered Uchenna. "If we try all the three, there is no way we cannot kill at least one animal."

"I think Uchenna is right," said Ugonna.

"Is the place where you saw the holes close to the school, so that we can go now?" Ugonna asked.

"It is not too close nor too far from here. I found the tunnels in the bush behind Akajiaku's compound," Uchenna responded.

"We will go now; there is no time to waste," Ugonna suggested.

"We will not go now because we are still at school. School is not yet over for today," countered Chibuogwum. "We can go after dismissal."

"Chibuogwum, what are you talking about. Don't you want to get meat to eat and even give to your mother to use to prepare food and make her happy?" Ugonna asked.

What Ugonna said to Chibuogwum about giving the meat to his mother sank deeply into his heart, and he began to find going to kill the big rats immediately as very important. He thought that if he left the school and went and killed the big rats and give to his mother, it was one of the ways to start fulfilling the promises he had made to Uloaku, his mother. He believed that if Uloaku saw him brought home an animal that he had killed and gave to her, she would be glad and praise him and say it was an indication that he would do well in life. In fact, it would show that he was going to be a great person if he grew up, for a bright day begins in the morning. A child who would be useful in life in his adulthood must show it at infancy, he thought. "I must prove to my mother that I am determined to be a successful person and bring joy to her," Chibuogwum said to himself in his heart.

"Ugonna, I am beginning to see reason in your suggestion," Chibuogwum said to Ugonna "I think we have to go at once. Let us go to the classroom and collect our school bags, because school might have dismissed before we return."

"Now you are talking like a wise boy," Ugonna commended him. "As you have said, we will go and take our bags before the break is over. Uchenna will lead us to the place because it is him that knows where the holes are."

"Let us go immediately and stop staying here wasting our time," Uchenna urged.

"We'll make sure we leave without anyone seeing us, especially the teachers," Chibuogwum warned.

They all rose and began to move towards the classroom to collect their school bags and get out of the school without permission. Sadly, before their arrival to the class, the class teacher was already in the class. Also, as soon as they entered the classroom, the bell sounded, signaling the end of the break period, thus forestalling their plan to sneak out of the school. Therefore, they were disheartened and dismayed, mainly Chibuogwum.

"My plan has been shattered," Chibuogwum said in his heart. "But nothing spoiled. Tomorrow is yet another day."

On their way home after school, the three friends discussed how to go about their game of killing big rats. Each of them contributed his idea. Ugonna said they should go very early in the morning, and after get prepared and go to school.

The other two rejected his idea, saying that it was impossible, since they had plenty of chores to do in the morning before coming to school.

Uchenna on her own part said that it was better done during break, that they should leave the school as soon as the bell for break was heard. This was also pushed aside by the others, referring to their experience recently as a reason.

Lastly, Chibuogwum suggested going the hunting after school dismissal. Uchenna and Ugonna also did not accept his idea. They said that if they decided to engage in the activity after school and did not come home on time, their parents might get worried over their safety. They also remembered that they always had a lot of works to do for their parents at home in the evenings, after school.

Truly, they were confused and stuck regarding what to do next. They went on making various suggestions. At last, they agreed that they would not come to school the next day. They resolved to deceive their parents by telling them that they were going to school, but would actually go to bush to search for big rats to kill. Their plan was to prepare as if they were really going to school. They would put on their school uniforms, but have other dresses inside their school bags, which they would wear when they enter the bush to hunt. Then, when they estimated that school had dismissed, they would return home, pretending to have gone to school. It also came into their minds that they might be asked where they had got the animals from, if they eventually succeeded in killing any. To this, they had another intense and serious deliberation and came to the conclusion to tell them that they killed them when they were working on their school farm.

Having concluded all their plans for the following day, they agreed on where and when to meet before engaging in the next day's secret activities.

CHAPTER
TWELVE

The following day, Chibuogwum woke up very early in the morning. Immediately he got up, he began to prepare as if he was going to school. He washed his face, cleaned his mouth and went to stream to fetch water. When he went to the stream to fetch water, Uloaku used the time to warm food for him to eat when he returned. Chibuogwum took his bath in the stream, and then came back home with a bucket of water. He poured the water into the water pot and thereafter, went to the dining room to eat his breakfast. After eating, he left the dining room and went to get ready for school. But he was not going to school; he was only going to search for big rats to kill. He wanted to wear his school uniform to deceive his unsuspecting mother.

He went into a room and put on his school uniform. He collected his learning materials – textbooks and exercise books, ruler, pens, cleaners, etc, into his school bag. He held the school bag on his left shoulder and looked at himself in the mirror that was hung on the wall of the room and was happy and contented with the way he dressed. Then he came to Uloaku who was in the sitting room, getting ready to go to work and announced to her that he was leaving for school. After that, he left. Chibuogwum had already smuggled out machete the night before.

Uchenna, Chibuogwum and Ugonna met at the appointed place and time. The first person that arrived at the place was Chibuogwum. Within ten minutes after his arrival, all the two also came. They all came in their school uniforms, for they had each deceived their parents to believe they were really going to school.

The three rugged friends hurriedly got prepared. They put off their school uniforms and put on ordinary clothes, made for the day's activity of going into the bush to hunt for rats. Their preparation there to go to the bush to kill big rats was quick, because they feared that someone might see them and report them, either to their parents or to the school authority.

"We have to get ready immediately and get out of this place before someone meets us here and report on us, either to our parents or to the teachers", Chibuogwum said.

"Chibuogwum, you are very right," Uchenna agreed. "We have to leave as quickly as possible."

"Yes, let's hurry up," Ugonna said. "We must not take risk. If we are seen here, all our plans are ruined. Not only that, our parents and teachers will punish us and call us disobedient and arrogant children."

They got ready quickly and left the place. When they entered the bush at the backyard of Chief Akajiaku's house, Uchenna showed the other two the hole he had previously spotted. Without delay, they cleared the surroundings to locate hidden outlets. They found four outlets and the entrance. Then, they cut sticks and used them to block the outlets, leaving only the entrance open. They got some quantity of dry leaves and blocked the entrance hole, lit the leaves and began to fan it, making the smoke to go into the hole to disturb whatever was inside it. This particular task of fanning the smoke was done by Chibuogwum, while the others stood alert, watching to see when the rat would burst out and then kill it. It was Ugonna that did the work of clearing the surroundings and locating the outlets, while Uchenna cut sticks and blocked the outlets.

In the school, morning assembly had begun, but Uchenna, Ugonna and Chibuogwum were not seen. Their class teacher wanted to ask other students why they were not at school, but he decided to let that be, for they might still come to school, but must truly come late. He was slightly worried about why the three friends had not come to school.

After the assembly, the students sang as they marched to their various classrooms. The JSS two students, as others students did, which was the class to which Chibuogwum, Ugonna and Uchenna belonged, also marched into their classroom, singing jubilantly. They entered the classroom and Mr. George, the class teacher, called the students' names from the register, but only Chibuogwum and associates were absent.

"Chibuogwum Okereke," called Mr. George.

"Absent," answered the class.

"Uchenna Igwe."

"Absent."

"Ugonna Chigozie."

"Absent."

Mr. George's worry about the absence of Chibuogwum and his friends from the school that day increased. Therefore, he thought it was proper to know why it was so.

Chibuogwum and his friends were deeply devoted to their work. Chibuogwum had fanned the smoke into the hole for some time, and the rat in it felt disturbed and uncomfortable. It sought to escape through the outlets only to find out that they were all blocked. Chibuogwum and his friends were glad as they heard the sound from inside the hole, for it was an assurance that something was actually inside the hole, that their labour would not be in vain. The rat attempted to escape through the various outlets, but they were all blocked. Then, it moved towards the entrance to escape. Chibuogwum, Uchenna and Ugonna easily felt it coming. They got ready to catch it alive, but Chibuogwum suggested that it was better they use the cutlass rather than bare hands, to avoid danger, for it might be a different thing that was coming out.

The animal that was in the hole, defiled all dangers which it might had noticed were around and burst out at a great speed, attempting to escape. Ugonna used his cutlass on its head, and it died instantly. The three friends rejoiced. But that was not all, there was yet sound being heard inside the hole, indicating that others were still inside the hole. This time, it tried to get away through one of the outlets only to be disappointed to see that it was blocked. It attempted to run away through the entrance hole, where Chibuogwum and his companions were waiting for it. What happened to its brother also happened to it, this time by Uchenna. Chibuogwum and his friends were so elated. They thought they have finished. But wait: some sound was still being heard in the hole. As the first two had done, it also attempted to escape through the outlets but failed. It burst out forcefully, pushing out the leaves that were used to block the entrance, as it attempted to escape. The boys were taken unawares. The animal ran out of the hole to search for a safe place. Because it was daytime and the smoke had weakened it, it ran slowly and Chibuogwum and his companions pursued it, determined to kill it.

The three boys ran after it with visible determination to get it, dead or alive. And because of having been exhausted completely, the animal cowed after trying to run away from its pursuers for some minutes. Then Chibuogwum hit it on the head with a stick, and as it went through the throes of death, Chibuogwum picked it up and used his machete and bled it and it died as blood gushed out from its throat.

Chibuogwum, Ugonna and Uchenna were overjoyed because of their propitious activity of going to kill rats, which they had engaged in. The three friends were so glad and decided to go home, for they had achieved their goal of killing rat – three for that matter, which meant that each would get one rat to take home. They shared the rats- one for each person and made towards home.

In the school, Mr. George was determined to find out what was wrong that made Chibuogwum and the other two students to be absent from school that day. He sent the class prefect, Nnanna and his assistant, Uzumma to go to the boys' houses and find out if there was anything the matter. Nnanna and Uzumma complied quickly and hurried to the boys' homes, but met their absense. It was at around twelve p.m that they went, which was the time they were in the bush killing rats. That was the reason they did not see them. Nnanna and Uzumma came back and reported their futile journey to Mr. George. He decided that he would go to their houses himself after school dismissal to find out what was wrong.

As soon as the school had dismissed, Mr. George moved straight to Chibuogwum's, Uchenna's and Ugonna's house one after the other. He did not see anybody when he arrived at their various houses. Then, he decided to go home and rest and wait until the next day when they would come to school and he would know why they were not at school the previous day.

Chibuogwum arrived home in the evening. His mother was already at home before he arrived in his school uniform, which he had once removed before he went to kill the rats and now put it on again. He looked so dirty and tired. He was holding the rat in his right hand, a machete in the other and on his back was his school bag.

"Good evening, mum," Chibuogwum greeted Uloaku as soon as he entered the house.

"Welcome, my son. Why are you so weak and your clothes and body are not clean?" Uloaku aksed.

"We were working on our school farm. That is why I am tired and returning late," answered Chibuogwum.

"Sorry my son," Uloaku said sympathetically, "You need to eat, take bath and then rest so that you can regain the energy you lost. Did you hear?"

"Yes mother," replied Chibuogwum.

"And what is that in your right hand, my son?" Uloaku asked.

"It is my own share of some rats I and my friends killed while we were working our own portions on the school farm today," Chibuogwum lied.

"A whole rat for you alone, my son? What about other students? Did they also get a full rat as you?"

"No, mother," replied Chibuogwum. "It was only me and my two friends that killed the big rats – three in number and we shared it among ourselves, one for each. Other students were not involved in killing the rats."

"You are a good child, my son," Uloaku remarked. "You have shown me that you will truly be a useful and an important person in future. Now, give it to me, let me keep it so that I will later prepare it and use it to cook delicious and sumptuous meal for you, your siblings and myself."

"Mother, did you remember that I promised that I will take adequate care of you if I grow up and become an adult?"

"That's what you said, my child,"Chibuogwum's mother, Uloaku said gladly. "And I can see that you have begun to fulfill your promises. I am very proud of you."

"Thank you, mama. This is just the beginning. More will still come. From today, I will prove to you that I mean every word I said in the promises I made to you."

"Oh, my child, I am proud of you. At your age, you have already started showing me that you are going to be a source of joy, consolation and comfort to me. You have proved that as my only son, you are going to bring me comfort and do for me what your father would have done for me if he was alive. You are so valuable to me."

"Thank you, mama," Chibuogwum said happily, "for trusting in my ability to make you happy in life. Just as I have promised you, I am determined to fulfill my promises. I will not disappoint you."

"I thank God for you, my only son. "As it's usually said, a good day starts with a bright and sunny morning."

"That's true, mother. A person who will be rich in his adult-hood usually begins showing it at infancy."

"And that's what you've started to do. This rat you have killed is an evidence that you are heading towards greatness. It is unusual to see someone of your age who can kill a rat and bring to their mothers as you have just done."

"Mother, I know that as an only son, I have to make great efforts to make you glad by being of help to you."

"Good boy; God will bless you for me," Uloaku said smilingly. "Now bring the rat and let's go in so that you will eat, bathe and rest." She collected the rat from Chibuogwum and they went in.

CHAPTER THIRTEEN

Chibuogwum and his friends Uchenna and Ugonna came to school the following day in good time. They had been told by their fellow students, especially their classmates that their teacher, Mr. George was worried about their absence from school the previous day to the point that he sent the class prefect and his assistant to check on them in their various houses. Thus, Chibuogwum and his friends realized that they must have explanations to make about why they did not come to school the day before. So, they gathered to discuss what they could do and what to tell their teacher.

"What are we going to tell our teacher is the reason we did not come to school yesterday," Chibuogwum asked Uchenna and Ugonna as they gathered.

"Let us tell him that we accompanied our parents to farms to help them," Ugonna suggested.

"I don't think he will believe that," Uchenna said, "because it sounds impossible that all three of us would go to farm with our parents the same day. I suggest we tell him that we were sick and so were unable to come to school. I think that is easy to believe."

"It is the same thing as what Ugonna had suggested," Chibuogwum remarked. "It is impossible too to believe that all of us would fall sick at the same time."

"Now, what is your own suggestion about what we will tell him?" Ugonna asked Chibuogwum.

"I think we should follow Uchenna's idea," Chibuogwum answered.

"Why did you say that? "Ugonna asked. "You just said that it sounds impossible."

"Yes, that's what I said," Chibuogwum answered. "But I have just carefully considered the suggestion and I came to the conclusion that it is the best thing we can tell our teacher is the reason we failed to come to school yesterday. We will tell our teacher that my uncle came to village the day before yesterday and gave me a kind of drink I had never seen before and that I brought it to you and we drank it and it made us sick. We suffered from diarrhoea, that's the reason we did not come to school yesterday."

"It is an excellent idea," they chorused. They all adopted that suggestion made by Chibuogwum as what they would tell their teacher if they were asked why they were not present at school the previous day. Chibuogwum was so glad that his idea was accepted.

When Chibuogwum and his friends and other members of their class had entered the classroom, the class teacher called their names from the register. Chibuogwum, Ugonna and Uchenna all answered, "Present sir" when their names were called. The teacher Mr. George felt relieved as he heard them answered "present sir", knowing that they were still alive and healthy too. Wanting to know why they were not at school the day before, he asked them:

"Chibuogwum, why is it that you and your friends did not come to school yesterday?"

"We were sick, sir," Chibuogwum replied.

The teacher was surprised. "All three of you sick at the same time? Is that possible?"

"Yes, sir," Chibuogwum answered. "My paternal uncle came to village from the city two days ago and gave me a type of drink that I had never seen before. I shared it with Uchenna and Ugonna, my friends and it caused us diarrhea. That's why we did not come to school."

The teacher believed what Chibuogwum told him without doubt. "I see. Is that why you were not able to come to school yesterday?" Mr. George said. "I sent the class prefect and the assistant to go to your houses and find out what was wrong. They came back and reported that you were not at home. I even went to your houses myself after dismissal and also met your absence. I'm so sorry for your illness. I hope that you have fully recovered?"

"Yes, sir," Chibuogwum replied, "we are now okay."

Chibuogwum and his friends all went back to their various homes after school had dismissed, full of happiness that they had succeeded in lying to their teacher. As a result, they considered themselves clever, having deceived their teacher into believing what was not true. They were so happy that they had avoided the punishment that the teacher would have leashed on them if he had found out that the reason they did not come to school was that they went to bush to hunt for big rats.

Before Chibuogwum arrived home from school that day, his mother, Uloaku had already prepared a delicious soup, using the meat of the big rat that Chibuogwum had brought back home and given to her, and gari to use to enjoy the soup cooked with the meat. Mr. Okereke's younger brother Chinweuba, Chibuogwum's uncle had visited and gone back shortly before Chibuogwum came back from school. When he arrived, Uloaku gave him a piece of the meat and told him that it was Chibuogwum who killed it and brought to her.

"I have always said that the boy will achieve great things in life, "Chinwuba said. "Look at what he did. I am very proud of him. This is evidence that he will be a great person. God has marked him out for great achievements in life."

"That is true, my husband. I have truly suffered, and my prayer is that God would use him to wipe my tears and bring joy to me. Of course, he had already promised me that. I believe that God would help him to fulfill his promises. When he brought the animal to me, I told him that that was a sign that he was truly determined to ensure that he fulfills his promises to me."

"Indeed, he will if he continues like this," Chinweuba said. "He is your only son, and God will make sure that he uses him to make your life enjoyable."

"That has always been my prayer, my brother," Uloaku replied. "He will bring comfort to me. I am glad that he has begun fulfilling his promises. Chibuogwum is beginning to show that he will do great things in future."

"Yes, and that should not be a surprise to me, because he takes his father's characters; he resembles my brother. In fact such is in our family blood," Chinweuba said.

"It is not my husband that he resembles, neither does he resemble me," Uloaku responded. "His bravery and determination are his unique and peculiar characters."

"Whether you believe it or not, it is the characters, attitudes and behaviours of our family that the boy possesses. Every one of us started to make great achievements when we were at very tender ages. Even our fathers, grandfathers, great-grandfathers and their fathers' fathers all did the same."

"I am not arguing that with you. What I am saying is that Chibuogwum is a separate and distinct individual, and therefore possesses his own separate, distinct, peculiar and private manners. And that's what makes him different from others."

"But remember that our people say that if a child does not resemble his father, he must surely resemble his own mother. It surprises me that you are saying that Chibuogwum resembles neither you nor his father."

"I have not said that he did not resemble him in any way. At least, he takes after him in physical appearance."

"Not just physically, but also characteristically."

At this moment, Chibuogwum came back home from school. "Good afternoon, mother," Chibuogwum greeted his mother who was talking with his uncle.

"Welcome, my son," answered Uloaku.

"Good afternoon, Uncle Chinwe."

"Thank you my child. How are you? And how was school today?"

"I'm fine, sir. School was very fine today. Everything went well."

"Fine, I'm glad to hear that," uncle Chinwuba replied joyfully.

"Go inside and take your food and eat," Uloaku told Chibuogwum. "I used the meat you brought and cooked a very delicious and tasty soup to make you happy."

" I thank you, mother for taking good care of me," Chibuogwum appreciated. "You are the best mother I can ever think of having. And I promise to reciprocate by making you happy and contented when I grow up."

"I'm proud of you, my son. God knows that it is your desire to make things good for your mother, and he will surely help you do your heart's desires."

"God will answer your prayer, mother."

"He is a good child," Uloaku said to Chinwuba. "He loves me so much and is determined to see me become happy and comfortable in life."

"And he will surely do it," Chinwuba assured her. "God knows that he is your only son and he will help him. God knows what you're passing through and he will bring you rest and relaxation in life through him."

"Indeed, the boy knows that life has been so unfair to me. He once made great and wonderful promises to me. He promised me that if he grows up, he will buy me luxurious cars, airplane, helicopter, get me house help and said that everything I have lost in life and all my pains, he will correct. He said that he would make sure that God uses him to comfort me."

"As I see it, he will make it in life," said Chinwuba. "I will now go home." He rose to go.

CHAPTER FOURTEEN

As time went on, Chibuogwum no longer found joy in going to school. He and his friends began to do petty jobs and got some money to buy things that they wanted. Chibuogwum only went to school two or three days in a week and used the remaining three or two days to do some petty works to get money for himself and to give to Uloaku. He no longer cared about education. He engaged in numerous jobs and activities which included going fishing, killing various kinds of animals, etc. His mother, Uloaku accepted the money he gave her, which he made from the works he did, with joy and gratitude. She was not at all concerned that her son, her only son had stopped going to school. She was only contented that he was bringing her money, without thinking about how that would affect her son's future.

One day, Uloaku called Chibuogwum to ask him why he no longer went to school. "Chibuogwum, I have observed that you miss school always. What's wrong?"

"Nothing is wrong, mama," Chibuogwum replied, "It's just that I no longer want to go to school."

"Why are you talking like that my son?" Uloaku asked. "Have you forgotten the promises you promised me? Don't you know that if you don't go to school, you will not be able to fulfill them? Without education, you will achieve nothing."

"It is not so, mother," Chibuogwum cut in. "Whether one is educated or not, the person must become what God says the person will be. Take for example Chief Akajiaku. He did not go to school, and yet he is very rich, far richer than many highly educated persons in the community. I believe in God's destiny and plan for me in life."

"Well, you are right. Let it be done for you according to your wish. God will be with you. I know that whatever God has written about one's life, nothing can make it to be rewritten."

"Mother, have faith in me. With or without education, I must be rich and make you comfortable."

"Yes, my son, I believe that God is hearing our voices and will support your efforts."

"You see, mother, success doesn't depend on being educated. Whatever God has destined for one's life must surely come true. So, mother I no longer want to continue to go to school. I know that it's God that make one prosperous, not education."

"You are right, my child," Uloaku replied. "It is God that gives prosperity. If you don't want to go to school again, there is no problem. But the only thing I will want you to do for me is for you to first learn to read and write, at least your name."

"Mother, if that's what you want, I have already achieved that," Chibuogwum said. "I can write and do readings. If you doubt me, let me spell my name for you. C-h-i-b-u-o-g-w-u-m-–Chibuogwum. Then, listen as I spell my father's name Okereke – O-k- e -r –e-k-e – Okereke. Am I correct, mother?"

"You are correct, my son," answered Uloaku. "But you will have to exercise a little patience and continue to go to school until after this academic session. Then you can stop. God will surely do it for you as you wish it."

"Thank you mother," Chibuogwum thanked his mother, Uloaku. "It is God and destiny that decide what one would be in life, whether rich or poor."

As Chibuogwum and Uloaku were still talking, Chinagorom and Chimamkpam came back from school.

"Good afternoon, mother," Chinagorom greeted Uloaku.

"Welcome, my daughter," replied Uloaku.

"Good afternoon, mother," greeted Chimamkpam.

Welcome, my daughter. How are you people and how were your studies at school today?"

"We are fine, mama. Everything went smoothly at school today," Chinagorom and Chimamkpam answered simultaneously.

"Mother, have you observed that Chibuogwum no longer go to school these days? Why?" Chinagorom asked.

"Yes, mother I had meant to ask that question that Chinagorom asked," said Chimamkpam. "He is not doing himself any good by not going to school."

"How does that concern you?" Chibuogwum asked, interrupting her. "How does it concern you whether I am doing myself good or not? Is education a guarantee to success and progress in life? Is it necessary that one must go to school to be successful in life?"

"The way you reason will never help you," said Chinagorom. "Those that did not go to school when they were supposed to are regretting it now. Think well about what you are doing."

"Please, leave him alone; let him be," Uloaku said. "It is only God that dictates what one will become in life. There are many who are not educated, and yet they are the pillars of their families, whereas some who are educated are the shames of their families. So, as Chibuogwum said, education does not give success."

"Talk to them, mother," Chibuogwum said, supporting Uloaku. "They think that if you don't go to school, you can't make it in life. Think of how long it takes to get educated: Nine years basic education, three years in senior secondary, and four years or more in the university and one year for National Youth Service - a total of seventeen years. After that you are not assured of immediate employment. You do not know how long you still have to stay before you get a job. But if you use that long period of time to work or do business, you will know what you will achieve."

"You are right, my child," Uloaku said. "God is in control of all things."

"Whether you agree with us, or not, mark today's date, Chibuogwum will surely regret what he is doing now in future," Chinagorom said, trying to make them think. "He may be happy now that he is getting money, but later in life, he will regret his decision and will cry for it and say had I known."

"If that's what you wish for me, it is you that will have it," Chibuogwum replied angrily. "You will suffer and regret in future. You no longer have respect for me as your elder brother, Chinagorom. Why?"

"She is telling you what is true," Chimamkpam said.

"Two of you should stop that nonsense, or I will be angry with you. Don't you know that he is your elder brother, and that you should mind how you talk to him? And now both of you should go inside and don't try this nonsense another time. Whatever he will be in future is not your business; neither does it lie in your hands.

Chinagorom and Chimamkpam quickly went in, as instructed by Uloaku.

"Imagine such insult, disrespectful and indecent behaviour, mother," Chibuogwum remarked. "Is it their work to predict what I will be in future?"

"Never mind them, my son. You don't have to get worried. It is God that has the power to decide what one will be, not anybody nor education."

"They do not know that. Mother, I am so grateful that you talked to them the way you did. The trust you have in me and in

God's power as the ultimate source of success will not fail you. You will not be disappointed."

"I believe that, my son. They have left. Don't let what they are saying sadden you. I know that you will grow up to become a responsible man and fulfill all that you have promised me."

"Now, I hope that you have consented that I should stop going to school. I hope we have agreed."

"Well, I would have preferred that you continue to go to school until after some time, at least to acquire Basic Certificate. But since you no longer want to keep going to school, I will not dispute with you over that. I am not in God's place to influence your future. God will reward your decision."

"Mother, thank you for your understanding," Chibuogwum said. "Chinagorom and Chimamkpam will see that education does not mean prosperity. They must surely see me succeed. Let them continue to go to school, wasting their time. By the time they have finished school, I must have known what I have achieved."

"As I have said, I will not force you to change your mind. It is not humans that give prosperity, but God. My prayer is that God will be with you in your endeavours and pursuits. Of course, I can see that God is beginning to show that he approves of your decision by beginning to make you get money."

"I am very proud of you, mother. I will make sure that I fulfill all that I promised you if I grow up and become adult," Chibuogwum assured Uloaku. "Don't listen to what Chinagorom and Chimamkpam are saying. It is only God that decides what anyone will become in life. I pray that God will keep all of us alive to see what everyone will become in future."

"My son, I have told you not to be worried about what your sisters are saying. They are talking rubbish, trash. Never mind them. They will surely see that being uneducated does not prevent one from achieving what God says one will achieve."

At this point, Chibuogwum's uncle, Chinwuba arrived. Immediately he approached the house, Chibuogwum and Uloaku exchanged greetings with him. Chinwuba asked Uloaku how she and her children were. Uloaku replied that they were fine. He was satisfied to hear that they were alright and he said:

"I am glad to hear that you are fine and I can see that too with my eyes." He saw that Chibuogwum looked sad. So he asked what was the problem with him.

"You look unhappy, my son," Chinwuba said. "What is your problem? Why are you not happy?"

Chibuogwum said nothing in reply, because of the anger bottled up within him. Then, Uloaku decided to answer for him.

"It is his sisters; they insulted him," said Uloaku in response.

"What happened?" Chinwuba asked.

"My husband, Chibuogwum has decided that he will stop going to school. And when Chinagorom and Chimamkpam heard it, they became unhappy and told him that he would regret his decision in future. They said that if he is not educated, he would not make it in life, that education is the key to success."

"I think that they are right," said Chinwuba. "We should try to learn from other people's mistakes and avoid making similar mistakes. Evidences show that those who used the time they should have used to go to school and become educated to work and get money when others were in school, usually feel regret over their actions later in life. So, I will advise that you listen to them and make him to see the reason to continue to go to school. If he does not agree, force him to comply to your order. He should be corrected now; he should be made to know that his decision is misleading. To be honest, he will not make it if he does not go to school. Nowadays, it is educated ones who make it in life."

"I don't believe that, uncle," Chibuogwum interrupted Chinwuba, "success comes from God alone."

"Stop interrupting me," he said in anger. "What I am telling you is for your good. I thought the same way you are now thinking when I was a boy, and now I am seeing the negative outcome of it. If you don't go to school, you will end up achieving nothing. The many years that you will spend going to school scare you. That is the major problem most of you young ones have today. You think it is better to use those periods to work and earn money quickly. But at last, those who chose to go to school become far better than you. Left to me, I would not allow you to follow your decision."

"My husband, I really thank you for your advice," said Uloaku. "But I believe that it is God who decides what one would become in life, not education. There are some who are not educated, and yet they are very rich. Also there are many educated persons who are poor. So, I don't think that education is a guarantee to success. We should let him do whatever he chooses to do, and not try to make him take a different decision. If we do and he does not make it, he would blame us. But if we allow him to follow the course he chooses and he fails to make it, he will have himself to blame for it."

"Note that I am not trying to decide for him or for any of you," Chinwuba replied. "I am simply making a suggestion. But be certain that if you don't apply my advice and decide to follow what a little boy who does not know what he is doing says, you will surely regret it."

"Don't worry, Mazi Chinwuba," Uloaku said. "Besides, destines are not the same. Nevertheless, I thank you for your concern."

"All is left to you," said Chinwuba. "You are free to decide whatever you want to decide and do it."

"I am sure that God will be with us and bless us."

"Well, that's what you believe. I have spoken my mind. I came to know how you are doing. I will now leave. Where are Chinagorom and Chimamkpam?"

"They are inside," answered Uloaku, "Let me go and call them to come and greet you." She raised her voice and called: "Chinagorom! Chimamkpam!"

"Yes, mama," Chinagorom and Chimamkpam answered one after another.

"Your uncle is here," Uloaku informed them. "Come and greet him."

After a short moment, Chimamkpam and Chinagorom emerged."Good afternoon, uncle," Chinagorom greeted Chinwuba.

"Good afternoon. How are you?"

"I am fine," replied Chinagorom.

"Good afternoon, uncle," Chimamkpam greeted.

"I am happy to hear that you are all well. My advice to you is to take your studies seriously and obey your mother and do your domestic chores. Also, obey your teachers and do any home work they give you. With education, you can make it."

"Uncle we will do as you have advised us," Chinagorom assured Mazi Chinwuba. "What you said is true."

"Uncle, do you know that Chibuogwum has decided to stop going to school?" Chimamkpam asked.

"I will beat that your big mouth if you don't shut it," Chibuogwum said angrily.

"Is that what you are called here to come and talk?" Uloaku asked, grimacing at Chimamkpam. "You always like to start trouble. This your big mouth will land you in great trouble that you will not be able to come out of one day if you are not careful about how you talk."

"You should try to apply my advice," Mazi Chinwuba said. "If you do, it will be well with you now and in future. I will now go back."

Uncle Chinwuba departed.

"One day, I will beat you until you faint," Chibuogwum threatened Chimamkpam. "Do not worry; continue to talk rubbish. As mama said, your talkativeness will cause you big trouble one day and you will not be able to come out of it. It is then that you will realize yourself. Look at her mouth!"

"That's enough, Chibuogwum," Uloaku said. "She will not do it again."

"It is better she doesn't do it again, because if she does, she will not have the mouth to talk what I will do to her. Warn her."

CHAPTER FIFTEEN

F ew days later, Uloaku called her daughters, Chinagorom and Chimamkpam to the sitting room to talk to them.

"I called you here this night because of what happened few days ago, during which you insulted me and your brother," Uloaku began. "I chose to talk with you at night because I feel it's the best time to do it. I hope that you are listening to me very attentively?"

"Yes, mother," Chinagorom and Chimamkpam responded simultaneously.

"Good. Since you have decided that you will not help me get money to help to run this family's affairs but to go to school and waste your time acquiring education, with which you are not assured of employment, I have decided to withdraw my support."

"Mother, why?" they asked.

"Are you asking me," Uloaku replied in anger. "Your elder brother has decided to stop going to school in order to work to help me care for the family. And instead of being happy for it, you blamed him and said all sorts of nonsense to him. I have decided that from today, you will begin to see to your education. I will no longer be involved; I will no longer finance your education. What I will promise to do for you is to continue to provide you with food and clothings, which are the things I should do for you as your mother."

"Mama, this is not good," Chinagorom and Chimamkpam said at the same time in alarm.

"What is not good? So you want me to continue to pay your schools fees and die? I have made up my mind that you should stop going to school but if you must continue to go, be ready to take care of everything. I know that unlike Chibuogwum your elder brother, you don't want to help me. You want to see me suffer and die."

"Okay mama," Chinagorom replied. "But we can go to school and yet help you."

"Do you think that that will be possible?" Uloaku asked skeptically. "If you want to stop going to school and help me, do it. But if you want to keep going to school, know that my hand is not in it."

"Alright, mother," they replied. "We've heard you, and we will think over it."

"There is nothing to think about. What I said is final," Uloaku concluded. "Now, you may leave."

Chinagorom and Chimamkpam left.

"Education, every time education," Uloaku muttered to herself. "They don't care to know what it costs. They don't care about how I suffer to get money to pay their school fees. As I have said, they must discontinue going to school. Or if they want to continue to go, they must have to foot every payment. They want to kill me. Chibuogwum is not like that; he is good to me and helpful too. He works to earn money to give to me to help me." She sighed.

The following day, Chinagorom and Chimamkpam met to talk about what their mother had told them.

"Now that mother has decided that she will no longer pay our school fees and other things, what are we going to do? Because I don't want to stop going to school, said Chinagorom.

"And me too," replied Chimamkpam. "I must be educated, no matter the challenges."

"Sister, I like your courage. We must not let mother's indifferent attitude towards education to discourage or dismay us."

"Yes, we must continue to forge ahead and will never go backward."

"That is true, but what are we going to do? I am asking this question because we are still little children. We will not find it easy to get money for our school fees and other levies."

"That is why it is necessary that we talk about what we will do, and that's why I called you. I suggest that we will start to sell things after school in the evenings to get money for our school."

"But don't you think that it will affect our performances in the subjects?"

"I think you are right, Chinagorom. We need to make a new schedule to conform to our present circumstance and plan. That is the only thing I can think of now to do and get money for our education."

"Now, what exactly do you suggest we will be selling to get the amount of money that will be sufficient to pay our school fees and other essential levies?"

"We will begin to sell sachet pure water in the evening after we have returned from school. We will do the selling between 4:00pm after we have come back from school and 6:30pm. After, we'll return home to do our works in the house, rest and do our studies."

"That idea sounds good. But don't you think that uncle Chinwuba can be of help to us?" asked Chimamkpam. "He often speaks in support of our going to school."

"I don't know, but we can tell him and see if he could do anything about it."

Indeed it is important that we do so and see what would be the result."

As Chinagorom and Chimamkpam had decided, they later went to Mazi Chinwuba and told him of their mother's decision to stop giving them money for their education and paying their school fees. They also told him what they had planned to start doing in order to get enough money for their schooling. Uncle Chinwuba was moved. He was glad that Chinagorom and Chimamkpam were determined to go to school despite the challenges. As a result, he made up his mind to help them. He volunteered to be paying their school fees and other levies and school uniforms, while they would buy exercise books and text books themselves.

Chinagorom and Chimamkpam were very happy as a result and they thanked Chinwuba for his gesture. They promised him that they would take their studies seriously, to show that they were grateful. Further, they promised that they would not forget him when they grew. They decided that they would do any work for him to express their gratitude to him for his benevolence.

Chinwuba was much impressed. He told them that he was only doing what he was supposed to be doing. He said that Okereke, his late brother was a good brother and that anything he was doing for his children would not be considered to be too much on his side. He went ahead and let them know that he would treat and love them as his own children.

"What I am doing is my duty," he said to them. "Okereke was my brother. It's a pity that the Devil did not allow him to live and see you grow up. I loved him so much when he was alive and I even still love him, and that love that I have for him, I will also show it for you."

"Thank you, uncle for all that you have said," Chinagorom said.

"We are so grateful to you, and God will continue to bless you," said Chimamkpam. "He will surely grant you all your desires."

"As I have always said, your father was my brother. He was so good to me when he was alive. I don't think there is a better way to reciprocate but to love his children and do all I can to ensure that you succeed. I am disappointed that Chibuogwum decided to choose a course that will earn him had I known at the end. On the other hand, it gives me joy that you have chosen the right path. It may appear rough and hard now, but later in future, you shall reap fine fruits of your labour. My advice to you will always be that you must not allow anything or anyone to be an obstacle to your determination to keep going to school. Don't let anything you may encounter in future to discourage you. You have seen that your mother is no longer interested in your education. She wants you to stop school and start doing works and be bringing her money as Chibuogwum your brother is doing. But Chibuogwum and his mother will surely regret it in life. That was what I did when I should have been in school and learning something that would be of use to me. When I was young, I stopped going to school and used my time to work and make money. I was acting like a big boy. I was very proud of myself because of the money I got, and some other children envied me and a few of them joined me," said Chinwuba.

He paused and looked at them and saw that they were listening to him with great interest. He discerned that his advice was going deep into their hearts. Then he went ahead.

"I was with plenty of money and I boasted to others because of it. I thought that I was making it in life and enjoying my life. But see the result. I am now poor but those who were not getting money as I did at the time are now rich and are engaged in good works and are well-paid, enjoying themselves. They envied me at that time, and now I am envying them. If I had known, I would have used those times and concentrate on my education and forget everything about making money. I have learned my lessons and have vowed that I will never allow anybody related to me to tread the same path that I took. I now cry whenever I see my mates who are successful. It pains me."

"We are sorry, uncle," they chorused.

"It has happened already, and it can't be reversed. All I need to do now is to make sure that you, who are still young and are related to me, do not make the same mistake I made."

"We will take all your advice to us to heart and apply it," Chinagorom promised on behalf of herself and Chimamkpam. "We will make effort to make it in life."

"Whatever you do, my children," uncle Chinwuba continued, "always bear it in mind that taking the short and smooth road to success does not pay. You will certainly end up in sheer disappointment. If you want to do well in anything you are engaged in, you must be patient and walk on the rough and long way to success. Don't let anything to distract or sidetrack you."

"Uncle, we have heard all that you have said," Chimamkpam assured Chinwuba, "and we will follow your advice to the best we can."

"Yes uncle, we will put our best effort to make sure that we make it," Chinagorom added.

"Indeed if you do, it will truly go well with you, my children. I will always make myself available to render help to you in any area you would need my help. Be free to come to me and tell me if you want anything from me. As long as I live, I will ensure that I do everything I can to see that you do well in life."

"Thank you so much, uncle," Chinagorom thanked Chinwuba. "We are very proud of you."

"Uncle, we are very appreciative of all your helps," said Chimamkpam. "Uncle, we have to go now."

"Yes, uncle we will now be on our way," Chinagorom said

"Alright, my daughters," replied Chinwuba. "As I have always advised you, don't follow Chibuogwum's way. He may think that he is enjoying now, but future will tell. Safe journey, my children."

Chinagorom and her sister, Chimamkpam left uncle Chinwuba's house and went back to their house. They were happy because of Chinwuba's willingness to help them in their education and for his invaluable advice to them. They were more determined to go to school no matter the challenges.

CHAPTER SIXTEEN

Chibuogwum now totally quit going to school and completely focused on working to get money for himself and to give to his mother, Uloaku. Uloaku was so happy for the money that her son was bringing to her. She thought that by doing so, he was fulfilling his promises to her. And since Chinagorom and Chimamkpam had decided to continue to go to school and not to begin working and bringing her money, she felt they were of no use to her, unlike Chibuogwum. She was very much proud of him, and always praised him.

Chibuogwum was now fully engaged in his work to get money. As a result, he began to keep company with all kinds of persons, mainly those who are older than him. He started to misbehave and to live a rugged life. Those with whom he associated taught him all kinds of bad behaviours. He even stayed out of home for days and would not come home. Whenever he came back, he often returned with money and other things. Uloaku would be so glad and would not be bothered to ask him where he had been or what he had been doing all those days.

Mainly, he worked as a bus conductor, but sometimes, if he did not have anyone to work with as a conductor, he would be found carrying loads for passengers at motor parks and also helped drivers who were looking for passengers to get passengers, and after would be paid. Within a short period, he became used to such works and sleeping outside most time, and would not care to go home. And any time he came home, he won't stay long. He would just drop what he brought to Uloaku, his mother and hurried out at one. Uloaku did not care about all of these. She was only satisfied with what she got from him.

Chibuogwum also started to pursue girls. Sometimes, he would take them to cheap and local hotels and buy things, like drinks and meat and foods for them and also slept with them. He nearly spent all his money on them. While at times, he would prefer to bring them home, and any girl he brought home would stay with him for three days or more. Uloaku would not ask who she was or where she came from. She would relate with her as if she was her daughter-in-law. She showed no concern over her child's waywardness and lawless life style.

Meanwhile, Chinagorom and Chimamkpam were busy going to school. They began to do as they had planned. Every evening after coming back from school, they would get pure water and go out to sell. From doing so, they got money to solve some of their educational financial needs. They suffered and worked strenuously in order to make sure that nothing would prevent them from going to school. Uloaku saw all this as foolishness and hated them as a result.

"Good afternoon, mother." Chinagorom and Chimamkpam greeted Uloaku as they returned home from school one day.

"Are you greeting me," Uloaku replied in anger. "Is it only greeting that I will get from you? Will your greetings give me money to buy things to take care of myself and feed the family? Can it buy me clothes?"

"Mama, don't worry. In future, you will see the benefits of what we are doing now. But now, you may not see...," Chinagorom answered.

"Shut up your mouth and listen to me," Uloaku shouted, interrupting her. "I'm not talking about future; I only care about the present time. You should stop going to school and work to help me and yourself and the entire family. Education does not pay. Or if you can't work, go and get married. You are talking about the future which I don't know if I will still be alive to enjoy your so-called benefits of going to school."

"Mother, don't talk like that," said Chimamkpam "You will live to enjoy all your children."

"Story! Do you think that education guarantees success? If that's what you think, let me tell you, education doesn't pay. I will advice you as I have always done, to go and work and help me as your brother, Chibuogwum is doing or you get married."

"Mother, all these you are suggesting to us now may bring you only temporary gains, but in future you will regret it. It's better that you exercise patience and support us in our efforts to go to school, because it will be of lasting gains in future. It is good for us to learn from others. We should not make the same mistakes that our fathers and their fathers made."

"So you have got the mouth to talk rubbish to me anyhow? You think you are wiser than your mother that gave birth to you. You have grown wings to insult me; you have got the mouth to preach to me."

We are sorry, mama. It's just that we don't want to make..." Chinagorom begged.

"Now, I think the discussion is over," Uloaku concluded. "You are free to go inside and put off your school uniforms." Then she said sarcastically. "You still need to wear them and go to school so that you will become rich in future."

Chinagorom and Chimamkpam wearily complied and went in.

Apart from chasing women, Chibuogwum was also involved in drug abuse. He learned to use hard drugs from those he associated with. They smoked marijuana and Indian hem and made use of other emotion-altering substances and drugs. At times, they would be arrested, incarcerated and fined by the police, only to be eventually set free to do more. He had become addicted to hard drugs, that he was always in trouble with the police; that he was almost becoming like their customer. On many occasions, Chibuogwum fought and got injured and came home to be cared for by Uloaku, who cursed those that fought her son.

However, Chinagorom and Chimamkpam had completed their secondary school and were about to enter university. Fortunately, uncle Chinwuba who had lived true to his promise to help them at the time they were in secondary schools, also promised to assist them go to university. One day, they went to Chinwuba's house to tell him about their ambition to go to university. After welcoming and entertaining them, Chinagorom and Chimamkpam told him the reason they came.

"Uncle, we came to tell you that we are about to take our JAMB examinations," Chinagorom said. "But the problem we face now is lack of money."

"I have heard what you said," Chinwuba replied. "How about your brother, Chibuogwum?" he added.

"He is just managing. In fact, it has not really been easy for him," Chinagorom answered. "He has been from one problem to another."

"What kind of problems?" Chinwuba asked in surprise.

"Many kind of troubles, both police troubles and fighting with people."

"What could be the reason for such ugly development in his life?"

"Uncle, Chibuogwum now lives a wayward life. He now smokes and indulges in pilfering. And these attract police's attention to him and they arrest him from time to time."

"Now, you have seen why I insisted that you must go to school. I'm sure that by now, Uloaku must have begun to regret her allowing Chibuogwum to stop going to school. I have always said that I will do my best to sponsor your education, and I will not relent in fulfilling my promises. How much is the fee?"

"Forty Thousand Naira each," Chinagorom and Chimamkpam replied simultaneously.

"Come next week and I will give it to you."

"We are so grateful to you, uncle for all your help. We don't know how to put our gratitude to you into words. The only thing we have to tell you is that God will richly reward your good works," Chimamkpam said.

"Don't mention it. I'm only doing for you what I'm supposed to be doing for you. Come next week and you will surely get the money for your JAMB fees, ok. I will do all I can to see that you make it in life."

"Thank you so much, uncle," said Chinagorom. "We'll never forget all that you've been doing for us as it concerns our education. We will be leaving now, sir."

"Alright, please greet your mother for me. Make sure that you always do all you can to make her happy for I know that by now, she must have begun to feel regret that he let Chibuogwum stopped school. Don't remind her of the mistakes she made. Only put your best effort to succeed so that you'll make her happy later in life. Continue to study hard. Goodbye."

"Goodbye, uncle," they said and then left.

Chibuogwum continued to enter from one trouble to another. Now, he had got one of the girls he had affairs with pregnant. The girl, whose parents had thrown out of their home upon learning that she was pregnant, now came to live with Chibuogwum's family. It was Chibuogwum who was now living in the city that sent her to come to the village to live with Uloaku. It was Uloaku that solely took the responsibility of taking care of the girl, while Chibuogwum remained in the city, living a destructive life style. Whenever he returned home, he would only bring little sum of money and small quantity of food stuff, so little compared to what Uloaku spent feeding the girl and taking care of her in other ways. But any time he was returning, she would give him many things, like gari in large quantity, which were far greater than what he had brought when returning from the city.

Uloaku now had started to feel regret over her decision to allow Chibuogwum to quit school when he was a boy, against her daughters' and brother-in-law's advice not to let the boy stop school. She felt the weight of the responsibility of taking care of the girl that Chibuogwum impregnated and brought home to live with her. Not only that. Whenever Chibuogwum got into trouble, she was the person to pay for his release.

"Oh look at how I suffer, God," she lamented. "Must I continue to suffer without seeing anything good? Look at the type of troubles that Chibuogwum brings to me these days through his evil life-style. He always brings one trouble or the other to me. I never knew that this is what Chibuogwum would later become in life, despite all that he promised to do for me. I am beginning to understand that he behaves the way he does because he did not go to school when he was supposed to. If I had not allowed him to quit going to school, maybe by now, he must have got a good job. These troubles would not have come. Now, all the money that he gave to me before no longer comes. He is a source of woes to me now, instead of joy. Although Chinagorom and Chimamkpam, my daughters don't give me money, they don't bring troubles to me or make me sad, neither. They live quiet life. In spite of the fact that I refused to sponsor their education, they are doing well. They have taken their SSCE exams and are successful. I have also learned that they are planning to take their JAMB examinations and get admission into university. If I had known, I would have not listened to Chibuogwum's decision to stop going to school. I would have invested all my resources into my children's education, and the result may be positive in future."

CHAPTER
SEVENTEEN

U loaku now felt tired of caring for the girl that Chibuogwum impregnated and brought home to her. So, she decided to talk to Chibuogwum about it when Chibuogwum visited the village one day. On this particular occasion, Chibuogwum brought nothing, and worse still, he had big injury on his head, which he sustained during a fight with fellow arrogant youths.

"Chibuogwum, I called you here to talk with you," Uloaku began. "I know that you are listening to me."

"Yes, mother I am hearing you," Chibuogwum answered wearily. "Go ahead and tell me what you want to tell me."

"What I want to tell you is that what I am getting from you is not what I expected, neither is it what you promised me. You have been a source of troubles to me. You have truly afflicted me. Look at the girl you brought home after you have impregnated her. You dumped her here for your old and poor mother to take care of her, while you remain in the city doing nothing but bringing troubles to me to solve. You see Chimamkpam and Chinagorom, they are good children."

"No! mother, stop it," Chibuogwum interrupted her. "So they are now good to you and I am now an evil child? Let me tell you, mama you are the cause of my predicament. You allowed me to go astray. You allowed me to stop going to school when other parents were making sure that their children are educated."

"Shut up, this bad child," Uloaku shouted at him. "Are you not the one that chose that you would no longer go to school? Did I make the decision for you?"

"Stop talking like that, mother," replied Chibuogwum. "Didn't you know that I was a child at that time and did not know the implications of what I was doing? Didn't you know that you shouldn't have allowed me follow my decision. You should have known better. In fact, you are the cause of everything. You are the one to be blamed for everything that is happening now. You should have forced me to continued going to school, rather than listening to what a child that did not know what he was doing was saying."

"So you are now blaming me for what you did to yourself? If I had done the opposite, you would have said that I am a bad mother who does not want her children to do what they want to do. If you had gone to school because I forced you and you did not succeed, you would have said that I am the one who misled you."

"Mother, whether you agree or not, you are the cause of everything. Just take a look at how I am. I'm suffering and entering from one trouble to another, while my mates are engaged in well-paid works. You denied me education."

"You are the one who denied yourself education. It is what you chose for yourself. Didn't your uncle, Chinwuba advised you against what you were about to do? Tell me."

"And you opposed him and sided with me. You should have supported him and followed his advice. No, but you followed what a small child that did know not his right hand from his left hand was saying. Because I was working and bringing money to you at the time, you were blinded against looking into the future and seeing what such decision would result to. Had I known, I would have heeded uncle Chinwuba's advice and continue to go to school. Now, see what my decision which my mother supported has done to me."

"That's not what I am here to talk about. I called you to tell you that I am tired of feeding the girl that you impregnated and brought to me and taking care of her in other ways. As you can see, I am not getting younger. At my age, this is not what I am supposed to be doing. I should not be caring for you and your girl. Rather, you are the one that should be caring for me. It is not good that I would take care of you at childhood and also repeat it at this time that you have grown and are supposed to take care of me. Not only that, you brought a girl you impregnated to me to make me suffer and die. Chibuogwum to be frank to you, I am ashamed of you. You now have the courage and the mouth to tell me that I am responsible for your failure."

"Mother, I will keep saying it over and over again that you are the one that made me go the wrong path when you were supposed to tell me that what I was doing was not good."

"Now, listen to me. I will no longer be feeding the girl. I am getting old. You are the one that should be taking care of me, and not the other way round. You can take her to the city to live with you or you'll be bringing enough money to take care of her. I am tired. She is almost due to be delivered of her baby."

"To tell you the truth, I am not in the mood to talk about it now," Chibuogwum replied.

"You are not in the mood? So you want to see me continue to suffer until I die?"

"Is it not what you deserve? You did not correct me when you were supposed to."

"I have seen that you've grown to talk to me anyhow. Now listen to my final decision. I will no longer continue to feed her here. It is not my duty. You will now start doing that; you cannot kill me. God will not allow it. This is not what I expected to get from you. I will no longer be feeding her. You are the one who is supposed to be taking care of her, not me your old mother."

"Mama, you are still young to do that," Chibuogwum countered. "After all, what have you done for me as your son, your only son? Did you train me in school? Tell me."

"You are not ashamed to talk the way you are talking." Then, she repeated Chibuogwum's statement, like a little child. "Did you train me in school? Look at his mouth. Are you not the one that stopped yourself school? Now, this discusion is over. My final word to you is that I will never spend a dime on her again, period!" She left Chibuogwum and walked away.

Later, Uloaku called the girl that Chibuogwum impregnated, whose name was Nkechi, to tell her that she would no longer be taking care of her.

"The reason I called you here is to tell you something very important," Uloaku began.

"What is it, mama? I am listening."

"As you can see, I am no longer a little child. I am growing old, and therefore, it is appropriate that I should relax at my old age and be cared for by my son and my daughter-in-law, not the vise-versa."

"I don't understand you, mama."

"Don't worry yourself. Very soon you will understand. Listen to me first, let me talk to you."

"Ok, mama I am listening," said Nkechi.

"Good. As I was saying, I am growing old, and now is the time for me to relax and be cared for by my children and not I taking care of them. My son impregnated you, and instead of taking care of you, he brought you back to me to care for you in order to make me suffer, despite the fact that I am getting old and have suffered so much in life. It is really unfair that I should continue to suffer training you until I die. I have already spoken my mind to Chibuogwum on this matter. I am truly tired of it all. All I am saying is that I am going to discontinue taking care of you. It is not my duty. It's Chibuogwum's responsibility to care for you since he is the one who got you pregnant. Either he takes you to live with him in the city, or he will be sending things to you from the city. I cannot promise you that I will continue to feed you and provide your other needs because it is not what other women of my age are doing, neither is it my duty. That's the reason I called you here to talk to you. I don't want you to be amazed if you see my behavior towards you changes. I hope you have understood what I said very well."

"I understood everything you said," Nkechi replied. "But you should know that it is…"

"There is no 'but', "Uloaku interrupted Nkechi. "I have spoken and it is final and what must be done. Can't you see that I'm no longer a young lady and that Chibuogwum, your boy is bringing me a lot of trouble? Now, in addition, he has brought you to me to make me suffer the more and die. That will never happen. Chibuogwum cannot kill me with his troubles. All these things that I am getting from him are not what he promised me when he was yet a boy, neither is it what I expected from him. Chibuogwum has disappointed me. He is now worthless." She paused and then said to Nkechi. "Now listen to me for the last time: My taking care of you ends today. Go and take care of yourself if Chibuogwum can't do that. I am tired."

"Mama, I am not going anywhere," Nkechi muttered. "It is your son that made me pregnant, and it is the duty of this family to care for me and for my un-born baby. If Chibuogwum is incapable to do so, you do it."

"Shut up, this bad child," Uloaku shouted at Nkechi. "I will never continue to do that. Let Chibuogwum come and do his duties towards you. You mouth is bad. You will go back to your house."

"I will not; I'm not going anywhere." Nkechi stormed out immediately.

"Don't worry. We shall know who is truly the mistress of this house, whether it is you or I. This nonsense is getting out of hand, and it must end today. Chibuogwum will not kill me with his troubles. God forbid it."

CHAPTER EIGHTEEN

Chinagorom and Chimamkpam had taken their SSCE examinations and their results were excellent. However, they did not take their JAMB examinations the year they were supposed because of financial problem. That was the reason they had gone to Chinwuba's house to tell him about their intension to take the JAMB examinations, during which he promised to assist them financially.

As Chinwuba had promised them, he paid their JAMB fees. Chinagorom and Chimamkpam were elated that uncle Chinwuba fulfilled what he promised them. When the JAMB results came out, they were successful. In fact, in their various departments, they were among the candidates who scored highest marks. Chinagorom chose to study Law, for it had always been her desire to be a lawyer. While Chimamkpam chose accountancy, because she wanted to work in banks.

Immediately after they had obtained their JAMB results, they went to Chinwuba's house to show him the results. Chinwuba was so glad that they came and he welcomed them warmly and cheerfully said:

"You are welcome, my good daughters."

"Thank you, uncle. Good afternoon," they replied together.

"How are you? Sit down," said Chinwuba.

"We're fine," they answered simultaneously as they sat down on a double seat in the sitting room.

"How are Chibuogwum and your mother?"

"Uncle, to tell you the truth, Chibuogwum and mother are not happy at all. They often clash these days," Chinagorom replied.

"What might be the cause?" asked Chinwuba.

"Chibuogwum blames mother for his failure in life. He said that mother did not make him go to school when he was supposed to. But mother always tells him that he was the one that made the choice himself, and that he should not blame anyone for what came out of it. But Chibuogwum always maintains that mother should not have allowed him to follow that decision of his, for he was only a boy at the time and thought and made decisions like a child. He often tells mother she is the cause of his failure, but mother denies being responsible," Chimamkpam explained.

"All these things that are happening now, I spoke about them and gave my advice, but Chibuogwum and his mother rejected all that I said and treated me as a fool. Now, see the results. If they had listened to me, all this would not have happened. I am proud, very proud of you, my daughters that you followed my advice and persevered in your determination to go to school and succeed. I hope they have learned their lessons, but I am not glad that they learned them in bitter ways."

"Uncle, we came to let you know that our JAMB results are out," Chinagorom told Chinwuba. She then gave Chinwuba the results. "See them, uncle."

He collected the results from her, looked at them and commented with satisfaction. "Very good and excellent too. You have both done so well. Keep it up. Congratulations! I'm very proud of you. Come and shake my hands."

Chinagorom and Chimamkpam went and shook hands with him, saying: "Thank you, uncle."

"Now what do plan to do with the results?" Uncle Chinwuba asked.

"Uncle, as you know, we would have liked to further our education, but as you also know, there is no money," answered Chinagorom. "We have no other person to help us except you, and you are getting old and we should not be bothering you with our financial burdens."

"Don't be worried. I will do all I can to provide money for you to enter university and graduate. You have made me proud, and I will make sure I do my best to help you achieve your goal."

"Thank you, uncle," Chinagorom and Chimamkpam said respectively. Then, they left.

As Chinwuba promised them, he gave them enough money to process their admissions into university. He also gave them the appropriate amount of money that would see them through in the first year. Fortunately, they got admission into the same school. Chinagorom was to study law, while Chimamkpam would read accountancy. Chinagorom and Chimamkpam were happy that they had achieved their aim of entering university. They took their studies seriously. Their uncle, Chinwuba supported them financially.

When Uloaku heard of their admission into the university, she was glad. She sent for them, and they came home from school to see her. They got admissions into Abia State University, Uturu. Uloaku and her daughters sat on chairs in the sitting room.

"My daughters, I heard that you have gained admission into university," Uloaku said to them. "I am happy for you."

"Thank you, mother," said Chimamkpam. "We are thankful to God who made it possible for us, and also to our uncle, Chinwuba, whom God has been using to support us financially."

"My daughters, I am sorry for the manner in which I have been treating you. I know that I am the one that should be taking the lead in supporting your education. I beg you to forgive me for all that I did to you – for not showing interest in your welfare. I did not know that I was doing the wrong thing. The money that Chibuogwum was giving to me deceived and distracted me from what was more important. Now, I have learned my lessons. Please, forget everything that I said and did against you."

"Mother, don't weigh yourself down with excessive guilt and remorsefulness. You're our mother, and so we have forgiven you," Chinagorom assured Uloaku.

"Thank you my daughters, for showing understanding. As you can see now, Chibuogwum, your elder brother has disappointed me. I trusted in him to make me happy in order to make up for all the long time I suffered. But I did not know that my trust was misplaced. Now, you two are the only hope that I have. It never came into my mind that Chibuogwum could turn into a useless person. All his promises to me are now a waste. I have seen how my child Chibuogwum has fulfilled his promises," Uloaku lamented.

"As we have told you, you don't need to worry yourself about what has already gone wrong. All we need to do is to look into the future and forget about the past," Chimamkpam said. "You are our mother who carried us in your womb for complete nine months and there is nothing you can do to us that we cannot pardon you."

"Thank you so much, my good daughters, for your soft-heartedness. Once again, I ask you to forgive me for all the things that I did to you."

There is no need to keep repeating it," said Chinagorom. "We have forgiven you."

Chinagorom and her sister Chimamkpam continued their studies at the university. Mazi Chinwuba lived true to his promise as he assisted them financially right from the first year until they graduated. In due time, Chinagorom and Chimamkpam batched their first Degrees in law and Accountancy respectively (First class honours.) With the result, Chimamkpam went to various banks in search of employment, and she succeeded and secured work as a banker in one prestigious bank in the city of Umuahia, with attractive salary. On the other hand, Chinagorom entered a Law school, and after one year completed her course there and was called to bar and became a full-fledged lawyer. After a few months, she was invited to work at the Ministry of Justice, Umuahia.

After about one year, they settled comfortably in the city. Then they brought their mother from the village to live with them. As for Mazi Chinwuba, since he did not want to leave the village and come to the city and live, they built a comfortable house for him in the village, hired a house help to be helping him in his domestic works. They also made sure that he had enough money and did not lack anything that money can buy.

On his own part, Chibuogwum also benefitted from his younger sisters. They properly married Nkechi for him and got him well-established in a lucrative business. After some time, Chibuogwum decided to enroll into an adult school where he obtained his Basic Certificate and later his SSCE Certificate. Later, he took JAMB and did so well and was admitted into university to study medicine. In due time, he graduated with good grades. He later went and got trained and became a qualified medical doctor. He worked at a federal hospital.

On one weekend, Chinwuba and Chibuogwum visited Chinagorom and Chimamkpam in the city of Umuahia where they lived with Uloaku, their mother.

"My children, indeed I am glad that you all have made it. I am overjoyed."

"Thank you, uncle," Chibuogwum, Chinagorom and Chimamkpam said simultaneously.

"Now I am a great man, I have a banker, a lawyer and a medical doctor. I am very proud and highly favoured. Now I'm free to make troubles with people, because I have a lawyer who will defend me in the law court," Chinwuba said playfully.

"And I too. Additionally, I will pray for sickness to come for I know I now have a medical doctor who will treat me," Uloaku added jocularly. "As for money, we will not lack it anymore because we have a banker amongst us. I am now happy and comfortable. It is not easy that all my children are doing well."

The children joyfully replied. "Mama, you and uncle are so funny."

About two years later, Chinagorom and Chimamkpam got married and were blessed with many children. Chinagorom got married to a man who was also a bank worker. Regarding Nkechi, she attended a nursing school and graduated and became a fully-qualified nurse and was employed in same hospital where Chibuogwum, her husband was working. They also later had children who as well thrived in life. Chinagorom and Chimamkpam jointly built a mansion in their father's compound and bought a car for their mother, who had returned to village because she was now old. They also employed a driver and got a girl who would be helping her in her domestic works. Chibuogwum also built houses of his own both in the village and in the city. Chinagorom, Chimamkpam and Chibuogwum always made sure that their mother and uncle, Chinwuba lacked nothing.

Later, Chibuogwum built a modern and well-equipped clinic in his village where sick people would be treated free of charge. On their parts, Chinagorom built a civic hall for her people, and provided a vehicle for farmers in the village to evacuate their farm produce from the farm to the village, because their farms were always far from where they lived. Whereas Chimamkpam established a school in the village and attracted the establishment of a branch of the bank she worked at the village.

As a result of these giant contributions to the community's development, their people held them in high esteem. They always made sure that anyone who needed their help got it. Everybody spoke well of them at all times. In due time, they were honoured with prestigious chieftaincy titles by the people of the village, performed by the traditional ruler and his council of elders, in recognition of their contributions to the community.

www.ingramcontent.com/pod-product-compliance
Lightning Source LLC
Chambersburg PA
CBHW022136150726
47992CB00002B/620